D1808167

HITLER'S BOAT

HITLER'S BOAT

A Novel

Pierre Turgeon

Published by Transit Publishing Inc.
Copyright ©2010 Pierre Turgeon

The reproduction or transmission of any part of this publication in any
form or by any means, electronic, mechanical, recording, or otherwise,
or storage in a retrieval system, without prior consent of the publisher, is
an infringement of copyright law. In the case of photocopying or other
reprographic production of the material, a license must be obtained from
the Canadian Copyright Licensing Agency (Access Copyright) before
proceeding.

ISBN: 978-0-9812309-8-6

Cover design : Francois Turgeon
Text design and composition : Benjamin Roland

Cover photo:
© Hulton-Deutsch Collection/CORBIS

This book is a work of fiction. Names, characters, places and incidents
are products of the author's imagination or are used fictitiously. Any
resemblance to actual events or locales or persons, living or dead, is entirely
coincidental.

Transit Publishing Inc.
279 Sherbrooke Street West
Suite#305
Montréal, Quebec
H2X 1Y2
CANADA
Phone : + 1.514.273.0123
www.transitpublishing.com

Printed and Bounded in the United States of America

To my dad

But Man must devote himself to his country
To what use is revolt and regret?
If its image is painted at the Unicorn pavilion
Its bones can die on the battlefield

Tu Fu (712-770)

This cry, it is resumed into one word that each French Canadian will understand, after being so long asleep: "Soul of Old Quebec, awake!"

Adrien Arcand,
Octorber 20th, 1933

Sunday night, the German radio, during a show destined especially to French Canada, announced that Hitler is offering it its full independence.

Jean-Charles Harvey,
Le Jour, June 29th, 1940.

PART ONE

NOTEBOOK ONE

I have decided to stop waiting for the right moment to talk, because it will most likely never come. I will also skip the inspiration. I await no pardon, nor from God neither from my master, only the peace that comes from a sincere confession. After six years of war, I declare armistice and I sign my surrender without conditions, in Berlin, behind the broken windows of the Empire Broadcasting Company (Reichsrundfunk), all the Büro Concordia services having already fled for Dresde, which was broadcasting in India, Caledonia, France, Norway and French Canada. Dismantled telex, typewriters and boxes of documents clutter the entrance hall.

Arms filled with scenarios, folders and gramophone records, the secretaries hurry towards the trucks and cars that are waiting in the yard. Looking for colleagues that I used to see everyday down the halls or in the bunker so full of confidence, I push open familiar doors to see but one dust covered chair and to feel a cool breeze coming in through a broken window.

The violence of the Soviet artillery forced us, sergeant von Oven and I, to hide in the basement. There is no more coal left to heat up the chicory; we are smoking our last Juno. And now, since the generator has run out of fuel again, Von Oven is cursing as he goes out to siphon diesel from the destroyed Panzer. So I have a few hours alone ahead of me. I use this time to commit a modest sabotage, despite it being deserving of the firing squad, so that my story may live on; I am writing on the back of these documents I was given to microfilm, in German, to better camouflage this administrative Teutonic prose from which I hope to extract my own story.

Perhaps my text will make it out of the surrounded city. No one knows who will carry these documents out of the bunker after we will have photographed them in the last remaining operational studio in Berlin. Requisitioned by the Chancellery!

Shivering in front of the microphone even with my coat, hat and mittens, I repeat that the organists are fighting via their intermediary the French Canadians and that a closer look on the West front proves they are occupying the most dangerous sectors. Then, changing the broadcast frequency, I play the role of my character, Gustave Chénier, partisan of the Independent Laurentie, forced to hide in forests near Quebec to escape the Royal Canadian Mounted Police. I am supposed to be broadcasting from there, near my hometown, and not from the center of the Third Reich, from this city now surrounded by one hundred and forty divisions of Marshall Joukov, with fifteen thousand pieces of artillery.

I slept in the ministry's basement; the enemy planes were hindering my sleep. How do I stop my right hand from shaking? This morning, I sent someone to fill the prescription for tranquilizers, specifying to go to Engel's. He is the only one capable (everything will be ready tomorrow); even the SS central pharmacy has a hard time getting some, because the factories and labs have been bombed. Order and tightrope walking are two of my contradictory specialties. No one knows one's face before one is born. The present is catching up to me. My corpse lays there, like rotten meat, a machine good for the scrap yard. The world has no other face, no secrets. Bliss and misery. The movement towards the mirror could accelerate if my situation became unbearable. I cannot bear myself anymore. Moses, it's ghastly!

I hide what I've written in a black folder and then I hold it against my chest, under my jacket with a snap clasp belt. I sleep a little and I go down to the green room to join Hofer. Sitting in a Louis XVI sofa, he is burning the family heirloom of his master Gœbbles, whom he'd just seen at a meeting of the heads of department, in the clay stove, his muddy boots dribbling all over the thick Turkish rug.

The flames engulf photographs of the Doktor at age seven dressed in a sailor suit; they draw black stars in the middle of his elementary school report cards. Hofer's pasty white skin, his small blue veins throbbing beneath his temples, his bloodshot eyes; all signs that he hasn't been sleeping: a reflection of my own appearance.

"*Exoriare aliquis nostris ex ossibus ultor,*" he whispers, stuffing more paper in before shutting the cast-iron door. No, the avengers will not want our bones, because we will all be incinerated. A bomb explodes nearby. The walls vibrate. Some debris falls on the photograph lying on Hofer's knees. With a swift movement of his hand, he clears the glossy surface. "Let us pretend that the color cameras our technicians promised us really exist. Let us make our suicide an act of propaganda. How would you do it?" I shrug and say, "I'd improvise." He grimaces and clicks his tongue. "Tutt! Tutt! You need cyanide."

Without a word, he takes a small vial from his tunic, the top cut off, and lets me smell the slightly burnt hazelnut aroma. Then he softly blows over the opening. "Listen to this music. I have already used it for my dog. Conclusive!" He bursts into laughter and looks at his watch. "I have to go retrieve more documents from the bunker. Make sure everything is microfilmed for tomorrow. Take all night if you have to." Then with a wink and a smirk he says, "I will arrange for us to get the sacred mission of saving these documents. There will even be enough room for your wife."

I avoid reminding him that I was the one who thought up the operation: redemption through literary eternity of Hitler's intimate work, jotted down by three stenographs as he drinks the chalice to the dregs. After many texts spewed during his seclusion in the fortress, following the failed Munich putsch, he is once again inspired by this Götterdämmerung. I had suggested to Hofer that these *Works of the Devil* be taken out of the surrounded city and transmitted to posterity before the Soviets could destroy them. And why not carry them to my far, vast and frozen homeland? I had not anticipated the Führer would continue to write the ultimate verse and the penultimate maxim, forcing us to wait until the very last moment.

The operation would allow us to survive while fighting in the ruins. When it comes to double-crossing, Hofer and I need lessons from no one. Neuman clicks his heels, another scribe who exchanged his writer's cramps for the Hitlerian salute. The precise moment when he stiffly barks "Sieg!" he is permitted to, like all of his colleagues, dissimulate a fart. The horrid smell follows me all the way to the window. I press my nostrils between the two wooden boards that have replaced the glass.

Outside the moon is full. Frozen fog hovers over the surrounding lakes. Easter will come late in this year of 1945. Metal shards fly off in every direction at a supersonic speed: missiles, bombs, and tracer rounds. Panzerfaust. The racket stops for a moment and I hear the wind in a pine tree; I can breathe in the smell of wet sand coming from the gardens; my childhood games in Quebec beneath the shadow of Wolfe's cannons. And then a single gunshot in the Tiergarten close by and the sound of the ricochet.

Hofer stands up in all his tallness and lifts his arms behind him like a crow ready to take flight, as Neuman stands on the tip of his toes to slide on the heavy military jacket Hofer has been wearing since his nomination as Obersturmbahnführer. Then they both leave for the bunker. I return to my office and continue to read the notebooks that pass through my hands.

Completely obsessed by the fate of his future corpse! Yesterday, Hitler sent Fegelein, his brother-in-law whom he suspected of wanting to give his funerary urn to the enemy, to the firing squad. Die, you filthy beast! Your agony is just being prolonged in a most obscene way. Was I the one to trace these lines? Yes, I who will finally show my true colors, in this defeat that is my victory.

I, who sees to the extinction of the hydra, something that has not been done. He could make it with Baun, his private pilot who is waiting for him in the Tempelhof underground hanger along with three long courier Junkers. Since the Biderman firm dug the longest labyrinth in history thirty meters below the chancellery's court, I knew the Fürher had chosen as decor for the final act this cold and grey snake, coiled on itself, surrounding three ministries in its concrete coils, and able to receive within its entrails, its most loyal partisans: its last victims.

And I remember what he wrote in his Bavarian fortress twenty years earlier: "If things go wrong at the instant of supreme danger, I'll disappear." Simple men don't kill themselves. He had probably already chosen his exit strategy. I tried to guess it through his aesthetic-political delirium.

I, Adolf Hitler, on the day of my fiftieth anniversary, I know nothing about nothing, not even if I am human. I have never directly seen my face. I have never spoken with any other organ than a tongue. Traduttore traditore. I am not sure I had parents, that people exist when I am not around, that I will disappear after my death. I would like to want nothing- to become heavy, frozen, and predictable. But there will always be a fraction of a second when I will not know what is going to happen. I have a nosebleed. I miss my dose of cocaine. It is dawn in Berlin. I await the Russians. I would like to be dispossessed. I would like to become a man without a history.

A mild conjunctivitis, most likely due to the wind and dust since there are a lot of ruins and debris in the yard. I was forbidden to read, but I do not follow this advice. I also refuse to wear a protective visor. Me, looking like an accountant! Obviously, the long hours spent studying maps are not helping. Before my incarceration in the fortress, I had broken my left arm, but I was able to recover the use of it through rigorous exercise. They want to steal my corpse, those traitors. And the Dachau ovens have been shut down! And those idiots from the Gestapo are letting everyone go: one moment, gentlemen! Allow me to go to the kitchen to fetch some ice for your cognac. And they disappear. The coffin is purring like a refrigerator behind my shoulder.

Ever since Stalingrad, I cannot get a hard-on. To distract myself, I would like to read all of Heidegger, or buy myself a medieval torture chamber. Do not tuck the tip of your tie in your pants, Kubizek would tell me in Vienna. Only peasants do that. At the height of my power, there was no longer a need for me to think. But now I have to and it is ruining my existence. But I still have treasures of cruelty, like Job on his mound of manure. And beneath that mound, a pre-prepared retreat. No one will notice. It is unfortunate these people were not good enough for me. I will take the subway at Grosse Stern station. I have a private entrance. A 10,000-meter gallery. No need to stick my nose out, to expose myself to captivity. They would stick me in a cage at the zoo.

The literary transposition can never hide the blatant reality. Has he gone completely mad? Perhaps. But the risk of his architect having built him an emergency exit that does not appear on official plans is too great. I transmit this information in codes during my show that Radio-Berlin insists on broadcasting to Canada, in a rigor mortis of its will for power.

"This is von Chénier speaking to you directly from Berlin. I do not apologize for scrambling your frequency to announce that the war is still going on, despite rumors of the contrary. Hidden for over two years in an abyss in front of Cap Eternité, our U-Boat is slowly making its way to the surface. Gurgling bubbles escape its steel hull, made to last a thousand years by a Bremen ship builder. Commander Kohl, who has already sunk twenty-three of your dinghies, informed us that his torpedoes are in perfect working condition. Remember people of Mingan, how your cabinets opened, how your peasant dishware shattered as it hit the rustic floor of your homes, how the thick and acrid air of your kitchen escaped through the shattered windows the night when, missing an escort destroyer, a torpedo hit the cliffs at the entrance of your insignificant harbor. History was flirting with you and you were trembling with fear. And so I tell you again, as on the glorious fall of 1941, people of Quebec, abandon your wives to the brutal caresses of our soldiers. Pack all of your belongings on ships and head towards the Old Country, up the majestic Saint-Lawrence, bigger than all the rivers in Germany, quickly before the U-Boat's ruthless periscope breaks the sea-green waters and sends you to join the crews of Charlottetown, Rivière-des-Prairies and Cap Chat. To those who would believe this is merely a bluff on our part, I will simply say that yesterday, at the Paspébiac Hotel, the band played Glen Miller at the end Our network of informants also told us that Mackenzie King spent the night in the arms of his darling mistress and that you should not believe the lies your newspapers print about our beloved Führer, who is a good catholic with a special devotion to the Virgin Mary."

End of transmission. On the other side of the Atlantic, in Montreal's listening center they are probably already bringing the recording of my show to my half-brother, Captain Perceval Perkins, who will decode it. What the Allies will do with this information does not concern me anymore. I return home to go to bed with Lizbeth in the basement of our villa where I have brought down our mattresses. We are freezing right to the bones beneath the whitewashed vault. I risk a glance out of the covers and a shiver quickly sends me back into fœtal position. I would love a hot soup, some peat bog for the living room stove and a sleep that would not be disturbed by artillery. Night moves very quickly on Earth, changing its hemisphere of shadows and nightmares, it remembers the cider that was drunk in the time of King Arthur, the cries of baby tyrannosaurs being born in volcanic swamps and the first plant cell.

NOTEBOOK TWO

New shapes, new cosmogonies. I am a V1 speeding towards the stars before falling on the toilet bowl of a London WC. I am the secret weapon of an evermore secret victory created by mad scientists. My flesh burns like the fuel of an intimate hell.

Arriving in Canada, my ancestor was almost right out of the cathedrals. He found himself under a sulfurous moon, in a country where wolves gnawed the crosses in the graveyards and where the pagan cry of the raven chased away the angels. His wife, tied to a chair, which her bloodstained skirt covered, had her eyes gauged out and her nails ripped off by the Iroquois.

His world, that had taken him ten years to build after his escape from La Rochelle, after the crossing on the Capricieuse on rations of rotten lard and a horizon populated by mosquitoes and Savages, fell apart. They tied him to a tree, while drinking the liquor they had stolen from a trading post, a young woman throwing firewood in the fire. Later, the burnt remains of Sir Chénier were exhumed for a good and proper Christian burial.

I was born in Quebec City in 1917, inside the fortified walls, in the shadow of the Saint-Jean gate. I played along the narrow streets, full of the smell of horse manure and filled with the echoes of trotting hooves, as though in the well-hidden hold of a fabulous stone galleon, birthing exactly where the river becomes sea, in transubstantiation as mysterious as the one of wine to blood. Gassed by the Germans, my father lost a part of his lungs, in the trenches of Ypres. I was three when he left the sanatorium and six when he came back from New York with a degree in electrical engineering, which allowed him to find a job as a junior director in a power station north of Quebec, in Saint-Gabriel, next to the Cartier River. This son of a doctor secretly thought of civil engineering as a social downfall, which he hoped to save by becoming rich at the head of a hydroelectric company.

My mother, Virginia Perkins, married him during a leave at the beginning of the war, breaking the ethics of mourning, since she had only been widowed from an Anglo-Canadian lieutenant for two months that had died next to my father during a bayonet charge. Feeling invested with the mission of consoling this protestant with magnificent red hair, he slipped the ring on her finger and loved her long enough to conceive me and then kissed her, leaving her and my step-brother Perceval, then five, to fulfill his duty as a hero of the Empire.

When he came back, he forbade his wife to see her family again and to speak a single word of English under his roof. This tyranny was not to last. Soon Virginia and Perceval left us to go live with my maternal grandfather. Hence, I was raised in French by nannies, while my brother was raised in English. During the holidays, I would spend entire days at the station, between the transformers and the huge sparkling spider of the rotary turbine, lying at the bottom of a fall. The catwalk shook, the machines' high-pitched rumblings tore at our eardrums like a plane about to take off. Perched on my father's shoulders, I held on tightly to his hair.

The fall's vaporized water refreshed our sun burnt skin. "Look! It will be all yours!" He let go of my ankles to embrace all the pylons with a wide gesture, with high voltage cables running at the end of their arms of truss; all this material that he had bought thanks to a loan from the bank. Jumping from one tree to the next, the ravens preceded us with their dissonant cries; drops of water fell from the still wet pines into the pond, their circles not easily distinguishable from one of the long legs of the harvestmen's jerky strides. I ran on the wet grass. The sun sparkled over the tips of the pines and the black and yellow pansies' petals surrounded the porch like a velvet carpet.

In the evening, my father, who wanted to start up his own business, was experimenting at the station. He was attempting to improve the turbine by curving the blades and putting them closer together and at midnight, he would try out his prototype, which often led to power failures. The nanny would light a candle in preparation, and we would bathe in its languishing, oscillating light until the resurrection of the 60 watt light bulb: a bright flash that would rip me away from my dreams and would reconstruct the living room around the filament standing in its inert gas. Angels would cross the walls, lying in the air with enigmatic smiles under their twinkling hair; beavers would smack their tales on the carpet with a crash. Thus, my childhood was spent in modern amazement. My dad was a carrier of light, a Lucifer whose magic would light up the windows of the department stores.

My war name of von Chénier I took from my ancestor, Jean-Olivier Chénier, who John Colborne's soldiers killed with two bullets as he was running from the Saint-Eustache Church, which was engulfed in flames. Because he was wasting his time in the med faculty, my heroic and hypothetic great-great-grandfather (our relation is still somewhat foggy) would have been better off taking Carl von Clausewitz's classes, who taught at the Berlin military school from 1818 to 1830. The Prussian general's theories would have taught him that during war "the probabilities of life replace the concept's extremes and absolute," sparing him the military humiliation of shutting himself up with his four hundred men in a catholic temple devoted to the second century's martyr, who died asphyxiated with his family inside a brass barrel under which a fire had been lit.

Even though he was a poor strategist, the independence chief did not deserve the Church's refusal to bury him in sanctioned grounds. Yet he did so, dishonoring himself by trying to humiliate one of our rare heroes. Witness to the clerical and warrior bunging, Lord Durham, previous British ambassador during Alexander V's court in St. Petersburg, and named dictator of Canada by a young Queen Victoria, he assured us we had no history, that we did not exist, and that our essence was purely virtual, the crown had to eradicate it to avoid more troubles in North America. This old defeat humiliated me each time I heard an order barked in English to the red tunics sporting black berets who stood tight rows on the grounds of the Plains of Abraham, in front of the monument of Wolfe, our conqueror, also in front of my grand-father, Colonel Perkins, and that I was not allowed to approach since the separation of my parents. I, along with my comrades, began to believe in a country that would belong to us, which I called Quebec.

That idea did not come from my father. Despite his Anglophobia, he was still a federalist and an antinationalist. He plugged his ears to his feelings of inferiority; he stayed deaf to the sounds of the independence sirens. But this Laurentian Odysseus wanted his own destruction, and he was dragging his son along with the wreckage.

While in this Berlin that is falling to pieces and where folks practiced the hatred of Jews, he was teaching me the hatred of our own people. This condemnation presented a prohibitive and metaphysical character, as it only targeted our provincial, even medieval, accent or the fatal corrosion of our words by English, or the syntactical deformities of our sentences, but also a lack of soul. So, this was a people come from sub-humanity, from cattle psychology, from marsh sociology, from a history of stupidity!

Even the French, he had the habit of saying, even a worker, poor and drunk, could express himself a thousand times better than the best Canadian orator. He would not deny that foam floated on this muck, that a thin intelligentsia would be on top, but it was much closer to a bowel movement than actual mind work. My father's cartography placed me at equal distance between inanity and void: either I knew what I was and I belonged to a herd of donkeys, or I would escape the pen, but no one – I first – would be able to tell what I was anymore.

Foreigners wouldn't find grace in his eyes either. From the insolent, uncultured and awkward English, to the narrow-minded, fanatical, cruel and cold German, passing by the impious, drunk and petty French, the greedy and cheap Jew, the fat and disgusting American, it was humanity as a whole he would reek thunder upon during meals, with an eye fixed on an inaccessible ideal and the other on the one that exasperated him through an elbow placed on the tablecloth, by a mouth that dared to chew. To escape his wrath and his slaps, I would turn myself into a statue, but absolute immobility would only agree with him for a moment, since I was to ingest the various foods placed on different plates, my stiff muscles condemning me to spill glasses, pitchers and saucepans. I would hold my breath as the stain, as outrageous as blood on the Shroud of Turin, got bigger and bigger, moving towards the edge of the table, following the fickle topography of the salt shakers and the

25

tablecloth's folds, to finally drip on the kitchen's linoleum: and so with the liquid puddle mixed the dry banging of drops against nape.

From the bottom of my triple abyss, human, national and familial, how could I have formulated a valid thought? I could not! Only the rosary occupied my lips to tasks that were not profane. Jesus dead on his cross! I spent my childhood adoring a corpse. But the true corpse was myself, and not the Christ made of plaster and bought during a pilgrimage to Sainte-Anne, nailed by my father's stare that would not kneel next to me, but rather leaned against the wall in the hall to rectify with a kick to the back of my thighs at any slackening of my devotion.

More than religion, it was military history that he proposed as a model to rip me away from our depravation. On the living room walls, portraits of Napoleon, Mussolini and Hitler contemplated their prey as they ripped through them with their teeth, as well as the supposed prominence of their jaws. A few havens – Beethoven, Hugo, Péguy – completed this pantheon of rare humans to have achieved thought. I was perhaps condemned to become fatal and fascist. But I was also learning the taste of freedom.

I realize that I am darkening my father. Grace be given to him: he taught me to spell, for which he felt a fanatical respect. His dictations were punctuated with ruler strikes on the fingers at the slightest error and I can still feel his hot breath on my neck as he bent down to better read in my notebook as I was hesitating on the letters to write, but not too long because inaction was also punished.

Admirer of the Führer, he signed me up for private German classes, which allowed me to hide from the friars at my college the religious doubt I would write down in my diary. Thus, it was with Nietzsche's words that, in 1935, I admitted to myself that I could not believe in God anymore. "Gott is tot," I screamed as I threw a large-rimmed hat soaked in ideas as much as in sweat through my student-dorm window, flying and following an elliptical trajectory before dropping on the snow.

The relative and the zero triumphed. With the Aquinian doctrine of numbers, the City of God was crumbling, like San Francisco in 1905, full of speculators exploiting the course of theological changes, not knowing that the ground was slipping away from underneath their feet. Through this breach, the total war was already being engulfed, art for art and "to live is to sell."

When I had the audacity to expose my Kantian critical proofs of the Divine existence, the friars locked me up in a small underground, in the middle of what was a hole that led to the sewers. They had placed my typewriter on a wobbly table. Surrounded by the nauseating smell, I had to write up an act of contrition with humility. I was afraid the naked light bulb on the ceiling would die out; I would then have to grope around for the door, trying to avoid the gaping hole without any other point of reference other than the freshness and smell escaping from it. I wrote nothing at all and they had to set me free.

Behind the glass doors of the boudoir that served as his dispensary, my father sat, deformed and multiplied by the cuts in the windowpanes. He was wearing a blue Marian uniform and an arm piece with a swastika. I was filled with shame. A cigar in his mouth, he was dreaming out loud. He would finance, he said, the printing of tracts for the National Christian Socialist Party. With friends, he would create a New Order. He brought me to assemblies. The marching of boots chanted the patriotic speeches in the parish halls: excited salutes, shirts wet at the armpits, plaster Sacred Heart on a pedestal on a Corinthian molding, with its Jewish arms in the air to bless his anti-Semite followers, bloodstained cassocks from the blows given by the flocks to the Communists freshly arrived from Poland or Italy. It all seemed even more ridiculous and pathetic since these tavern pillars were giving into the British branch of Nazism.

This political fever was a release valve for my father's rage at seeing his company crumble under debts. Fascism consoled his despair. The only thing sacred he knew was money, which flowed everywhere at an infinite speed, and the trajectory and mystery of which drew the universe, like marbles coming and going on paper. "Since I refuse to sell to them, he repeated, the English are killing me." When the bank reminded him of the loan, he emptied the drawers in his desk and burnt the plans of the new turbine, waited for the bailiff to fix the seals and then, without a word, his jaws tightly closed on his chewing gum, and he went down to the engine room. He grabbed the alternator's high-tension cable and charred to death in his tweed suit that smelled burnt. In the tension change of my room's light bulb, I could feel my father twitch under the 150,000 volt electric shock.

The world was leaking like an endless suffering. Thought in flesh, like a hook in a fish: pull the line patiently, the swift silver flash jumping over the foaming water, and the INRI Christian mystery, the virgin uterus. Touch his wounds; my father was back from the dead. With his calm and serene voice, his love fixed the order of the planets. He was crying beneath the linen shroud. Violence rolled at the back of the sky: the stars were cries. The calm water beneath the cormorant's sharp beak, sunfish were offering their entrails to the fateful omens. My father wrapped a black and white cloth around his left wrist; his smile resembled the slash of a sword in a bag of flour. In the cemetery, the bugs assaulted me on that torrid night of July.

Militiamen of the People's Army of Quebec crammed themselves on a raft: busted three-cornered hats, uniforms ripped to shreds and archaic rifles. On the grey beach, a block of foot soldiers like a porcupine of bayonets was waiting for them. A sharp order: Fire! And the craft held nothing but corpses that the current was sweeping away towards the sea under the fog. But the killers did not leave their post, in a unanimous gesture, they reloaded their weapons because another raft was now emerging, or maybe it was the same one with the dead that the fog would have mysteriously resuscitated. Fire at will! This scene repeated itself as relentlessly as the waves that would come to soil with red water boots of the wigged officer, my maternal grandfather, who brandished his sword to order the successive discharges.

In the celestial Quebec grand-place, translucent slabs made of a milky glass, would light up red when you walked on them, on Sundays, during family walks in eighteenth century costumes: bodice dresses, crinolines, sheepfold embroidered silk parasols and velvet frock coats with trimmings. Under each slab, lit from the inside by a light bulb, the severed skull of a combatant was telling his tale and that was there that I listened to my father's wax head, crying with truth, he confided in me that we were humans, also. No more, no less.

What a strange irony for the Quebec freedom fighter I had become: Colonel Perkins, my maternal grandfather who resembled General Wolfe, at least, in the few portraits we kept from the conqueror of the Abraham Plains. I myself had red hair and could speak English. For many, this hybridity was a sign of duplicity. "Sell out! Traitor!" they would say to me. Far from alienating me from the national cause, these insults just increased my fervor as if my zeal could erase my original sin. It was my father's race that I wanted to glorify and liberate; the race that my mother's family mocked through endless litanies, and which I had to bear in silence now that my mother had taken me back. "Frogs. Always grand gestures. Such emotions! Chatterboxes! No sense of business. And on the battlefields? Cowards. Cowards!"

My grandfather must have known what he was talking about since, in 1917, he had commanded a platoon in charge of restoring order in Quebec after the riots against conscription. He had the courage to order his men to fire on an unarmed mob. Fifteen dead on the pavement.

"French Canadian cowards!" he said, squinting his pale blue eyes behind the cigarette smoke coming up from his rounded lips.

On a spring morning when the Colonel was giving training commands to his troops, a huge icicle fell from a cornice and outright killed him. Obviously, God's vengeance against this Catholic eater. A widower, he left all his fortune to his only daughter, Virginia, who could continue sending both of her sons to boarding school, one Lutheran, the other Jansenist.

No more than her widowhood, this death didn't change much about her existence. She continued to have her vaporous beauty photographed in the Parliament gardens. I guessed her lover by the looks she would give the lens; on the bound snapshots she would show us during holidays.

At twenty, Perceval embraced his military career. Insolent face, fake Parisian accent, cricket, tennis champion, tea drinker, reader of Lewis Carroll, hunter and cold-water swimming enthusiast, he invited me to take part in a canoe crossing of a frozen river with him. In 1935, he left us briefly for the Far East and the Balkans as a military attaché and information officer.

The same year, I moved to Montreal where, with the help of a professor, I found a job as a journalist: dogs being run over, mediums and ectoplasm, smell of ink and sweat as the deadline approached, three pages a day for the little miseries of the little people, my name printed on thousands of copies. I would scrutinize human nature through the help of the brief news: murders, fights, drowning, riots; my ear glued to the phone, I would wait for the breathless hush of the night to calm down. On the river, dawn would crack just like a nut.

In my nightmares, naked bodies would form the letters of my articles: here a woman was straddling her lover who, standing up, extended his arms forward to represent an F; a young girl prostrated in front of an old man formed an E. Thousands of sweaty acrobats were contorting themselves into the letters of the alphabet, and a surge of Lilliputian orgasms determined the evolution of my narrative. I examined with a magnifying glass the faces of this human tide: mouth opened, tongue hanging out and wriggling, traits deformed by pleasure. The words were writing themselves, they pulled me, tied behind a chariot through a crowd that covered me in gibe and spit, arms pulled forward, wrists broken over the keyboard by invisible shackles.

With the help of a typographer, I illegally published a nationalist paper that we would make at night. I distributed copies at the gate of factories, ready to run for it if a policeman came near. After the invasion of Austria, it was obvious a crisis was brewing in Europe. I wanted to avoid my people sacrificing themselves again for the British Empire.

In August 1938, I spoke in a meeting at the Gesù. Around two hundred people came to listen to the New Nationalism speakers. From the stand, I argued for a new Quebec republic, layman and neutral. In the back of the room, agitators from the National Unity of Canada Party in swastika uniforms, jeered: "Communist! Go back to Moscow!" one of them said. Other opponents, Maurrassian nationalists, who should have opposed the Nazis' federalism, joined them by chanting: "Damned atheist vermin!" The booing forced me to get off the stand without being able to finish my speech.

At the back of the room, a woman of about thirty, wrapped in a shawl with a bell hat on her head, was waiting for me. "You're right!" she said in German. "But it's not enough. You need numbers." I dragged her outside the hall saying, "And even if the world was full of demons, we would succeed anyway!" She burst into laughter and answered, "Luther! My father is a pastor in Bremen. I know all those psalms by heart." In a clumsy German, I asked if she was interested in our national cause. "I have enough of mine! No, I came to rehearse for a concert later on." Amateur pianist, she earned a living as a secretary for the Montreal German Railway office. Her comrades were entering the hall that was now devoid of the crowd that had come to listen to the political debates. She invited me to come listen to her.

Instead of going back to my apartment on Saint-Denis Street, I went down to the port, and then walked along the Lachine canal. Barges were going up the locks to pick up cargo of wheat, cars and cannons from Detroit or Chicago. When I came back to the nearly deserted Gesù, the trio was playing Mozart on the stage where my "For a French-Canadian State" poster had been removed.

The pianist expressed the deep and gentle sadness of intimacy. Between each movement, her eyes would turn to the violinist before diving back to the keyboard, where fingers that I wanted on my skin were running, light as pleasure. She sang in silence, marking the pauses with a sigh that lifted her breasts underneath her red satin tunic. I listened enraptured, already vaguely in love with this Lizbeth Walle, whose name was printed in gothic letters on the program. Pale and thin, the skin of her face betrayed the slightest emotion as I deciphered her blood flow with a certainty I believed divinatory.

A tuft of red leaves at the top of a maple tree was already announcing the arrival of fall 1938, as if the music had accelerated the passing of time and of clouds that stretched under the setting sun. I invited Lizbeth to a neighboring bar. She agreed to give me an interview for my cultural review. She was taking small sips of cognac.

Living in Montreal for the past few months, she had arrived in New York in 1937, on board a zeppelin that had left Frankfurt three days before. In the first class lounge, she would play the piano for the rich German industrials that were on the flight to meet with their American counterparts.

"I gave a concert at the Rockefeller Center. From the bay window beneath the passenger gondola, I could clearly see the patrons from the restaurant, saluting us with their champagne glasses. Since then… badaboom! The Graf Spee exploded. The zeppelins are over! I will remain the only flying pianist for a long time."

She hesitated for a moment and then added, "Actually, I was accompanying my husband. He is the one who brought me to Montreal. He was working on a thesis on French Canada for Frankfurt University: Kanada, die schwäche Ritze des Britischen Imperium. In English: Canada, the secret fault of the British Empire."

"And now…?"

"He has gone back to Germany. We became estranged ever since his enrolment in the party."

This tale, which she recounted to me in German, fascinated me. It gave me access to a universe different from the bland and devastated one my father had left me with. These German words, which resonated so softly in her mouth, seemed to offer a shortcut to beauty and truth.

She took me to her hotel. The scent of wet asphalt followed that of wet soil, arranged in patches in the middle of an interior yard, then came the rancid smell of mold in the narrow stairs, the steps creaking as we went up to her room.

She left me in the living room with a glass of scotch and opened the taps of a giant bathtub raised on brass lion claws. She joined me a half hour later, lathered in oil and perfumes, her blond hair falling heavily on the white bathrobe that was clinging to her still wet legs. She broke away from my first embrace to pull me towards the bedroom where a life-sized angel statue was peacefully smiling at us, and I took her in my arms again, shaking with desire, falling on the bed. She said, "The bedspread…" and I stood up again, feverish, eyes half-closed, pulling away at my clothes in front of the partially opened window, before falling on the bed sheets where she closed her eyes, a moan escaping her painted red lips. Her arms in a cross over the bolster, she was shaking her head, biting her fingers as her stomach caved in.

Our affair lasted a few months, until she got pregnant. I proposed to her. But first she had to divorce her husband. She refused to tell me about him, except to say that, now back in America, he was working at the German Embassy. She reached him by telex and arranged for a meeting in Washington. Before she left, she warned me that she would get an abortion. She had gotten the number of a doctor whom the senators' wives had made quite rich. She curtly refused that anyone accompany her. She came back ten days later, still pregnant and not divorced, and declared, "losing our child would have meant the end of our love."

She never knew peace. A muffled violence inhabited her: she lived her life as though she were riding a wild horse, her heart beating. She seemed detached from her actions. From point A to point B, she had to fill the role that she had been destined to fulfill. We had a son, who was born with a cry of rage, like all children. It seemed as though she was trying not to love him, fleeing the apartment, and finally sinking into a depression that I attempted to relieve with a trip on the coast of Maine. While my mother cared for Christophe, we walked on the beach at night, in front of what she called her "sea of serenity," where not a single speck of dust moved in millions of years. But no stupor is eternal and soon thought would see to putting her back in her place, in front of this villa we had rented, and the waves that would be pumping up like long grey muscles.

War was threatening, it had already killed Lizbeth's grandfather twenty years ago, on June 7th 1917, at three thirty, on the Messina crest, along with the entire regiment, sent its warning by firing five hundred tons of explosives placed in a network of mine shafts dug up over ten kilometers by General Plumer's men.

On the dawn of September 7th 1939, the day after the promulgation of the law of wartime measures, a policeman friend called to warn me that I would be arrested during the day for my defeatist arguments, hindering the recruitment and success of her Majesty's forces, crimes I had rendered myself guilty of through my pacifist and pro-independence articles. As for Lizbeth Walle, her nationality being that of an enemy power, she would also be promised the internment camp.

Incredulous, I simply crossed the street over to some friends' house. Disaster! At noon, a Mounted Police van stopped in front of our apartment door. The red tunics with round hats climbed up the stairs and soon broke one of the windowpanes to the door to get into our home. Holding Christophe against her chest, Lizbeth told me with a strange smile, "I've seen this before... They're going to interrogate the neighbors now. We should leave." My mind was a blur from too little sleep and too much coffee; fear had a firm grip on me.

Lizbeth was the one who organized our escape. We retrieved the car that I had parked in an alley and we left for the bank. To avoid raising the teller's suspicions, I left a bit of money in my account. We had a few hundred dollars.

Christophe was playing with his mechanical bunny. "We have to leave him in your mother's care," Lizbeth said. I knew she was right. Still an infant, he could not travel in the precarious conditions that awaited us. My half-brother Perceval's house was located in front of a park in Westmount. I parked on the opposite side, beneath the quivering oaks, and I waited for him to leave the house, a cane under one arm. He cheerfully marched up the hill towards the Atwater street station.

The sun was heating the velvet back car seat with broken springs on which Lizbeth had laid a naked Christophe after breastfeeding him one last time. She bent over him, as he was wriggling and smiling, hiding him under her heavy blond hair and speaking to him in German. With his mouth open, he seemed to feed off her, for lack of milk, a bitter wisdom. Then, she wrapped him up in a cloth and handed him to me.

"Don't stand there in front of the door! Your son will freeze!" my mother cried. But I stubbornly stayed on the balcony. Over my shoulder, she saw Lizbeth, on the other side of the park, smoking a cigarette as she leaned on the hood.

"We have to leave for a while..." "Wait... Your brother could..." She took Christophe from me and held him close to her. I kissed them both. "Don't leave with that German woman!" she cried as I was walking away.

Already, at the Petawawa Camp, the Arcand and Lanctôt Nazis were about to trade their blue Marian shirts for a stripped outfit with a huge red circle on the back of the cap and the tunic to facilitate the shooters' task in case of escape attempts, choosing exile over rotting in the Ontarian forest with its anglophile and centralizing mosquitoes. I crossed over to the United States by a deserted and hilly Eastern Township road. We found ourselves in New York two days later. We lived in Brooklyn for a while at a French painter friend of mine, who had offered us his sofa bed along with the cans that filled his kitchen cabinets. We would breathe in fresh air from the security ladder; the metal blades of the steps left imprints on our thighs.

She was blocking her ears. "I'm listening to my blood flow. It's like it will never stop." Love pulled us together. We were going back to the beginning of the world, with the sun setting on the edge of the asphalt-covered rooftops, to burst in the dressing table's mirror, with the scalding coffee and burnt toast that we ate as we read the *New York Times*.

My mom, whom I would call regularly, refused to bring us the child, because she thought our situation was too risky. My brother's insistence on obtaining our address persuaded me that he was collaborating with the police. I answered that we had no fixed domicile. Finally, friends would confirm that they were attempting to deport us.

While I was looking for work in the press and translation bureaus, Lizbeth would often go to the German consulate to obtain an extension on her passport. One day, she came back with mail she had received from Berlin: a letter stamped with a bas-relief of Hitler's profile; a heinous clown mask with a fixated and menacing stare. She read, short of breath, fingers trembling, and then she burst out into laughter. She pursed her lips and could not stop the flow of tears.

"I send these writings to the flames!" she said in metallic French. She kissed the letter, folded it and slipped it underneath her corsage. "The future will emerge from the embers of our hearts! Heil!"

The works of her father, the pastor, had just been burnt in Germany's public squares. From a Dachau re-education camp, he wrote to her to tell her not to come back to Germany as long as the Nazis were in power. What little mistrust I had left had fallen; Lizbeth was one of the victims.

One night, Lizbeth convinced me to take her to the restaurant at the Rockefeller Center, where she had seen her first Americans from the zeppelin's gondola. The waiters in white vests with golden buttons brought dry martinis to the perfumed and diamond- covered patrons, faces floated over the ships that were trailing along in the distance on the Atlantic, somewhat tempting targets for the submariners, who still respected the neutrality, in theory, of these cargos supplying whole armies from the United Kingdom. "I arrived through there," She said as she pointed to the emptiness over us.

This luxury carried me to the first level of ecstasy. From the speakers, Mozart quartets played in the dining room, the matchbooks had Blake and Goethe quotations on them, the paneled walls were adorned with impressionist paintings.

She was magnificent and she wore a pearl necklace. I absorbed her musk perfume from a distance. Tall, she always seemed strong and self-assured, but while making love, she would crumble at my first touch, eyes closed, listless, hot and abandoned, brashly emptied of all her energy and will. She ordered tea.

A gust of wind blew and shook the 44th-floor windows. Only one colossal customer, who had just arrived, guzzled his vodka and smashed the glass on the parquet floor. A busboy cleaned up the mess without a word. Our neighbor lit a cigar. An angular face, strong eyebrow arches, and a hooked nose created deep shadows over the very pale skin; fierce eyes, as if mounted on ball-bearings in the middle of their sockets, were devouring the space around him, stopping on Lizbeth, who was pinching her nose because she was bothered by the acrid smell of tobacco. She pointed to the cigar, which he immediately stubbed out. Lizbeth smiled and said "Vielen Dank."

Her eyes flittered about the spectacular point where she met the other's gaze; her face lit up just like when she played a *fortissimo* during a sonata: the high point of a mechanism as complex and refined as the ones from the Nuremberg bell-tower's automated ringers.

Soon, she was talking in that rocky language that I loved in her mouth so much, but was still understanding with difficulty. She motioned toward me with her chin, and agreed. The other man handed her a card that she slipped in her bag, snapping the golden clasp shut. He rose, bowed, and clicked his heels. She pouted behind the veil of her velvet hat.

"That was my husband, Ernst Hofer," she told me. "He works for the New York Propaganda ministry office. I explained that you couldn't find a job as a journalist in the United States because of your opinions. He said he would like to meet with you."

Simple coincidence could not explain this meeting that Lizbeth had clearly arranged behind my back. I was furious. "I will never work for the Nazis. And I'll ask you to never speak to this man again!"

I immediately regretted my harsh tone. I've never had a worse enemy than my own volatile temper. Seeing her turn pale, I should have apologized. But I remained silent, awkwardness growing between us. She slowly stood, the tightness of her skirt forcing her to rock her hips, while one hand pressed the ivory cigarette case against her waist. Her eyes avoided me.

All at once, the fatigue from the travel, the fear of being arrested and the anguish of spending my last few dollars in this five-star restaurant all came together to drag me down and paralyze me as she walked away towards the lift. The other man tried to stop her by lowering his hand and throwing me an inquisitive glance, but she continued on her way. He left a large note to pay for the bill and hurried towards the exit, just in time to catch the lift and go down with her.

Convinced they would finish the evening in the same bed, devoured by jealousy, I walked towards Soho to console myself the best I could. When I came back at dawn, I ran into my friend who was reading in the living room, his head shining beneath the lampshade. He looked at me with pity.

"She waited for you all night without sleeping. She left about an hour ago with her suitcase. She said it was for the best."

I calmly placed my hand on the wall in front of me and smashed it with a heavy ashtray. Then, I collapsed onto the floor, whimpering.

"She didn't want to tell me where she was going. But she left this letter for you."

Scared by my violence, my friend stretched his arm to give it to me. I had to use my teeth to tear one end of the envelope. "Go back to Montreal; retract what you said to be pardoned. Save yourself and our son too."

I put the trench coat and wet felt hat back on. It was still raining. I took her umbrella, convinced I would find her quickly, completely soaked. I went back to all our favorite places: Central Park, the vending machine cafeterias, the little windowless bars, the cinemas with the floors sticky from soda. Sometimes, I thought I had spotted her, then a detail would become more apparent and I would realize it was a stranger I had mistaken her for from a distance. I realized with worry that I was haphazardly looking for my beloved in the biggest city in the world. I walked relentlessly, only stopping for a coffee and a sandwich at the end of a table with a view of the outside.

After two days, I was desperate: she had left the city no doubt. Her absence burned me. The eighteen months of our life together, the German lessons given from Schiller and Goethe, the trips to Quebec, the dinners at my brother's speaking of religion and politics, the days spent caressing each other as the cold burn of winter raged outside, the peace she brought me when she would lie on top of me.

My heart was ticking like a time bomb. I was only moving forward to not stay still, because a twenty-four-year-old man crying on the corner of the street might attract people's attention, but the one who walks in long strides hides his face behind his movements. I fumbled with the small wad of dollars at the bottom of my small pocket; I would soon not have enough left to eat, unless I sold the Packard, which I was barely using to save on gas.

A human being resembles nothing. He has no shape. To see this abyss that digs itself and sucks, one only needs to close his eyes. Beneath the illusion of order, one will feel the night reinventing fate at random. Already, on September 26, 1939, the day of Warsaw's capitulation, two weeks after Her Majesty had proclaimed a "state of war with the German Reich in our Dominion of Canada," my story had dropped down a block, like a dark and desolate star, gifted with a malevolent force of attraction.

In Manhattan, on the corner of 5th Avenue and 15th street, in the shadow of the monolithic Empire State Building, blew the most violent winds of the city. They were coming from the Hudson River, this luminous and milky rectangle between the metallic geometry of the skyscrapers; the winds were pouring in from Quebec, barely slowed down by the Adirondacks up north. They were weaving between the banks, the trusts, the holdings, the hotels, like the pipes on a gigantic organ, and they were freezing my face and my thoughts. Encased in a concrete block, a steel pole was vibrating and its tip was tracing obscure signs a hundred meters above my felt hat. A fall out of time, in a damned, somber, negative space; a reverse illumination, darkening. Everything that was stopping, had already stopped.

Before going back to Brooklyn, I decided to patrol the neighboring area of the German consulate in my car for a while. Ernst Hofer appeared from the corner of a building. His black eyes as expressionless, as balls of tar were darting through the crowd as if looking for a sniper. Of all the chances that have happened in my life, I consider this one as the most miraculous. Without it, I would have gone back to Montreal to raise my son and to become a loyal little British subject of Her Majesty. I stretched over the seat to open the passenger side door that the wind almost blew off its hinges. Hofer bent down and saw me; without hesitating, he sat next to me. "Herr Chénier! I would have so liked to talk to you the other night. You are looking for your wife? Disappeared three days ago? Tutt! Tutt!" He seemed surprised. Up to then, I thought he would have been aware of Lizbeth's departure.

It was the end of the day for the office workers. A policeman pointed his club at me: no parking! I started the engine, driving over newspapers that were fluttering here and there above the pavement like spooked bats. "I have to leave the New World soon," continued my passenger. "The Americans are forcing us to reduce our consulate workforce; they are accusing us of espionage. I am but a mere government official to Doctor Gœbbels. Poorly paid at that."

He looked at his watch. "I have a meeting at our consulate. Come with me. The clerk at passports might be able to give you more information." His lips were constantly twitching as if their discomfort was translated into words, as biologically trained as the songs of the whales.

Following Hofer's indications, I parked in the consulate's interior yard. The immense reception hall resonated with tons of rings, each one abruptly interrupted by an office worker as he brought the phone to his temple like a gun to blow his brains out. Our shoes pounded against the marble.

A low political mass was celebrated here with the telex plugged directly into the hereafter of Berlin, placed like a votive hostel.

Communications officers accomplished the mystery of translating the numbered cables in the correct order. Warned of our arrival by his secretary, Eckel, a balding, pot-bellied worker with almost no eyebrows came out of his office and stiffened for a brief moment, his arm in the air: "Heil Hitler!"

"Heil Hitler!" Hofer answered.

The two men conferred in whispers. The ceiling was rounded like a palate. I was already feeling the gastric juices around me. Eckel preceded us to the basement, behind a gate that opened in the purring of an electric engine. In a room that stank of coffee long forgotten on its heating element, Hofer asked me to wait for them a few moments. He only came back after an hour, leaving me to fear that my unfortunate approach could have harmed Lizbeth. I was simply hoping that she had remained in the United States, but upon his return with Eckel, Hofer confirmed my worst hypothesis.

"Too late! She has gone back to her Fatherland; her father's land was calling to her; Rheingold, oh Rheingold, like the mermaid's chorus at the beginning of Siegfried: an irresistible song for us, Herr Chénier. For you too, perhaps? We shall see. She had to go back. So Eckel stamped the papers, the Ausweis, the Pass, she took the boat for Bremen two days ago. Heartbroken! Without you, without her son. She did not warn you? Women can be so cruel sometimes. War leads to so many sacrifices. If only England had respected our desire for peace when we decided to bring the Germans from Dantzig back to the Reich."

As he was talking, his voice sounding like the buzz of a razor, I could feel on my wrists and my throat cold steel shackles that clasped to teach me the great alchemy, not that of lead to gold, but of suffering to pleasure.

"Our friend publicly laughed at the Führer in his articles," continued Hofer. "But his real hatred, he keeps for the English. And he would like to create a Republic of Quebec, without war and without violence."

He threw a pile of pamphlets I had written under a penname. "In a bucolic way, really?" Eckel asked, amused.

"I have studied your country a lot," Hofer said. "Typical little people politics! Quebec belongs to history's oubliettes, with the Bulgarian separatist kingdom, the Great Duchy of Burgundy and the Kurd Empire. Unless it finds itself powerful allies…"

I interrupted him: "Did you force Lizbeth to return to Germany?"

"The Reich has no power here, and a simple cultural attaché such as myself, even less."

"You lie! You could blackmail her with her father who…"

I stopped. Too late! By losing my cool, I had compromised Lizbeth. Hofer smiled.

"I had given her a mission. If she has betrayed the Reich, she will have to face the consequences."

They both stared at me in silence. And the look they were giving me, mineral and merciless, made me fear for Lizbeth. I decided to feign. "Excuse me. What betrayal are you talking about?"

"The other night, I charged her with the responsibility of giving you a job offer. The Reich wants peace. Just like you do. And since your government is forbidding you from promoting your pacifist and pro-independence ideas, we offer that you speak to your compatriots through us. Our Empire Broadcasting Company has become a real society of nations: Arab, Indian, Turk, Irish and Scottish separatists. All in a war against the British colonizer. Through you presence, Quebec would join the fight."

Without any hesitation, I dove into the abyss: "Who said that Frau Walle has not succeeded in her mission? I haven't come to a decision yet, that's all."

To buy time, I asked for more details on their proposition. As a Radio-Concordia host, I would get 1200 marks a month (800 American dollars). I would be allotted an apartment near my workplace, the Rundfunkhaus. My employer, the Ministry of Propaganda, could fire me with a four-month notice, but I would receive a full year of salary in compensation. I could keep my Canadian passport and I would be provided with a working permit that could also be used as a visa. I would be able to circulate anywhere in Germany. For trips abroad, I would need special permission from the Gestapo, In which case, I would be allowed to ask for my naturalization as a German citizen. As for Lizbeth, she would be given a position in Berlin in order to stay with me and help me adapt to the Reich.

In a barely covert manner, Hofer was using Lizbeth as a hostage. I preferred not to imagine what her fate would be like in a "re-education camp" like Dachau. I called my half-brother who agreed to take the Montreal-New York train the same evening.

The sun was hitting the dirty stained-glass windows of Grand Central at an angle. The train hit the buffer lightly before releasing steam, through which the first passengers soon made their way behind the Black porters and their elastic strides. As agreed upon, Perceval passed me by with a look of total indifference and got in a taxi that I followed. He stopped at the Taft, which he quickly crossed to join me in the Packard that I had parked near the hotel's rear exit.

I recounted my conversation with Hofer.

"They want you to be the French-Canadian voice of Radio-Berlin. Who would write your texts?"

"I would, but I'd have to submit them to the censors before broadcast." Perceval warned me about our apparently fortuitous meeting: Hofer had surely planned it all the way to the broken glass. Lizbeth was surely an agent under his service. Her rushed departure was surely a way to force me into following her. I must have been identified as a sentimentalist and easily influenced nationalist early on.

"Ernst Hofer is manipulating you to get you to join their cause. He's the first director of the Aussenpolitischer Amt, Nord Amerika. He comes under the official Nazi philosopher, Alfred Rosenberg and his special intelligence office, the Aussenpolitischer Amt (APA), attached to the organization of the Nazi Party overseas and Gœbbels' Ministry of Propaganda. He built himself an Empire within these organizations."

A spy? Lizbeth? Then she was lost if I didn't follow her quickly. She had not had the heart to complete her mission and bring me to Germany with her. Maybe she truly did love me? The separation from our son surely tore at her. Politics are made with good feelings. To liberate Quebec, perhaps we had to associate with the Nazis. Like the Irish.

"Don't do it!" Perceval said. But I thought this war would not last and the Germans could tear away some of the concessions from the British. No one, Perceval promised, not even his closest colleagues, would know that he had met with me. I drove him back to the train without telling him I had made up my mind to betray the Dominion of Canada.

"We will take care of your son," he said. I shook his dry, but brotherly hands, the ones of an enemy no doubt, but ones that would fight me face to face. Without this war between us, what a team we could have made!

While I was filing out the necessary bureaucratic formalities for my departure for Bremen, a dream haunted me. My son Christophe lay on a hospital bed, almond shaped eyes, and thin lips. He was wearing pajamas unbuttoned at his chest, he was hot, sweat pearled on his forehead, and he was wiping it off with his grey woolen blanket. Turning around, he let his bunny fall, with its long floppy ears, torn from being pulled on from the pain of moist and post-operative nightmares; the bunny on the linoleum stank of disinfectant. I bent over to pick him up, and I heard Hofer's voice behind me: "It's so stuffy in here! We need some air!"

He was throwing the window open. The outside air swept in like a frozen wave on a ship's deck. Instead of intervening, I stayed on my knees, snuggling my face on the bunny, its fabric moist from having absorbed Christophe's fever and delirium. In one swoop, Hofer heaved Christophe at arm's length, all soft, smiling and confident, and, moving towards the window, he hung him in the air, among the snowflakes. The little head fell back, mouth opened to taste the snow.

Suddenly, Hofer was whispering: "It's better this way," and he let him go from the fourth floor. As he fell, Christophe lifted his arms and his eye towards me, his father, bent over the window, he shouted: "I love you!" Instead of falling vertically, Christophe was gliding over the sidewalk and then, was flying over the rooftops. I then stepped over the windowsill and threw myself into the middle of the storm.

NOTEBOOK THREE

On November 9, 1939, I got onboard the Ernst-Günther liner for Gothenburg, Sweden. From there, a virtually empty cruise boat brought me to Kiel. A counter torpedo boat was setting out to sea between two DCA towers. Covered trucks were driving all over the piers towards the formidable Bismarck cruiser's massive silhouette. The entire German navy seemed to have assembled there, from the pocket sized Deutschland battleship, to the Gneisenau battle cruisers, along with fifteen submarines or so. We moored next to a huge dock, where an army of workers was sealing off a breach in the Köln's right flank in dry dock.

Lizbeth was waiting for me in the middle of a tight crowd that was hurrying to the pier to leave Germany. Instead of the bright colors she was fond of, she wore a poorly fitted grey suit that made her look fatter. Never before had her face moved me so much as under this pale winter light. I saw in it the only loving traits death could have. She ran through the customs gate before the guards could stop her and, in the moment of our embrace, she whispered: "What have you done? Go back, you still can! Look behind me!"

A little man in a black jacket was watching us. He had accompanied Lizbeth from Hamburg, where she had been imprisoned since her return. I grabbed her by the arm and went to stand in line with the other travelers waiting to fill in the disembarkation forms. I told her of our son's latest prowess, as told to me by my mother on the telephone before my departure from New York. I soon had the opportunity to test the power of the visa Hofer had given me, first with the customs agent who did not search my suitcase and then with the agent in civilian clothes who obeyed my orders before disappearing.

"I decided we were taking our holidays here. The air is fresh. And in the off-season, it barely costs anything."

She almost got angry, but then shrugged. As soon as she had arrived in Kiel, the Gestapo had arrested her for "treason."

"Don't laugh. Singing a forbidden melody, doubting the victory, displeasing a chief- that is all treason." A few hours before my arrival, she had been brought out of her cell and dragged to the port without any explanation. "You were crazy to accept Hofer's offer," she repeated.

In a common and tacit agreement, we decided not to speak of the war anymore. The seagulls were flying over the dunes. Our joy – inappropriate and almost obscene – did not want to die, despite the war; it discharged its electricity, which smelled like a storm, into our mortal bodies and it allowed us to seize the other in an ultimate thrust.

We had to stop ourselves from starting to laugh out loud on the grey streets of Bremen, crowded with young soldiers at the end of their leave. We took the train to Cuxhaven, a seaside resort on the North Sea, which was deserted at the time. The casinos and Gasthäusen stood in a row along the shore. On the horizon, the U-Boats stood out, these great steel sharks that opened their jaws to the depth of the Baltic Sea only to dive into the farther and colder waters of Greenland and the shores of my homeland of Quebec to rip up Canadian ships with their torpedoes.

Off-season. All the hotels were closed except for the Neue Liebe, this "new love" where we were staying. When the owner told us we were the only guests, I asked for a master key so we could change rooms every night. So there we went, from one room to the next over the ten floors of the tower that was being assaulted by the hurricanes blowing in from the sea, and when we would go to bed, no one knew where to find us. To reach us by phone, one would have had to call the one hundred and forty-two rooms, one at a time.

I had the impression of resembling a diver who trains to jump a little higher everyday, up to this altitude where you are no longer falling but flying, with the difference that I was traveling through time, and that my last jump, the one where I would wish for luck to be on my side, would furtively drag me head first and forever toward absolute sadness. How beautiful death seemed, at the Neue Liebe, in Cuxhaven, a few sailing hours from Hamlet's kingdom.

In the evening, we enjoyed oysters in the restaurant on stilts. We rose our glasses of wine from Rhine. We knew nothing of the war yet, except for the bomb dropped by a solitary Mosquito: the strike of a hammer, under which the city's granite skeleton shook, even through her body, Lizbeth's, as we made love.

She fell ill. Rolled in a tight ball under the covers, her right hand gripped my wrist tightly and her teeth chattered. Where her fever had dropped slightly, I turned the lights off in the room and went to sit by the partly opened patio-door above the sea. Night and fog enveloped us.

The next day, she felt better. She was wearing a green dress, the same bright shade as her eyes. Only a light redness around the sides of her nose betrayed her cold. Her hair was up on the left side, revealing a pearl on her ear, and fell to her shoulder on the other side. When resting, Lizbeth's beauty had something a little intimidating, but when in action, it was bewitching.

Our idyll, which actually got its charm from its extreme precariousness, ended that morning at breakfast when Hofer erupted in the dining room.

"Herr Chénier! Here I am at the exact time: German precision.... Gnädige Frau."

Very tall, he leaned to kiss Lizbeth's hand. He seemed to want to portray a last century British gentleman with his grey tweed suit and a gold pocket watch attached with a chain to his coat pocket.

I had not told Lizbeth about this meeting. I was still wondering whether or not they were in cahoots to drag the boundaries of Germany in me. I remained convinced that the meeting between the three of us, at the Rockefeller Center, was no coincidence, but a skillfully calculated ruse. I hoped the element of surprise would betray the real nature of the feelings Lizbeth still had for her ex-husband. On her face, I only saw a mixture of fear and disgust. She handed him a miniature battleship-shaped bun the bakeries were making. "Take a bite of this Graf von Spee. Unless you would prefer a little Bismarck? The English would surely like to eat one!"

He shook his head, and then winced, as from a secret pain, an ulcer perhaps, which sent him on a new line of thought like a horse that has just been whipped. "I have news from your father," he said to Lizbeth. "Not very good. He died in Dachau. Heart failure. My condolences."

She had already stopped listening to him. She opened the door to the terrace and leaned on the railing. He let out a deep sigh.

"One never knows how to word these misfortunes… And so here is the Pacifist with the lords of war. Very good! Berlin needs you. Oh! Not at the front, but on the radio waves, alongside the Irish, Indian, Scottish and Breton nationalists."

"Stand up!" He had barely gotten to his feet when Lizbeth slapped him with all her might. "There shouldn't have been a cardiac arrest! Our agreement is kaput!" I felt a strong surge of jealousy: this physical violence let on a great intimacy between them.

Ignoring the blood trickling from his left nostril, he lit a cigarillo and then, with a smug grin, placed a photo on the table between us. Our son was smiling from the bottom of a baby carriage that my mother was pushing between two snow banks in front of the Atwater fire station in Montreal.

"It was like the North Pole at your place last week," he said to me. "And you will never guess who took the photo. Freedom does not exist. To make history, you have to let your rage out of yourself. You, the weak people, you cross the Red Sea that roars above your bent heads. Us, we curse this God who slowly chews on our bodies in the saliva of time."

Lizbeth left us, sobbing. He had boasted to the Propaganda Ministry of my talents as a speaker and my sharp quill. I would have to convince my compatriots not to go to arms for the British Empire's lost cause.

I listened without batting an eyelash. The two-week romantic hiatus had come to an end on the shores of the North Sea. I had preserved our tranquility to the very last moment, because I knew it was the eye of the cyclone that would take us away.

He suggested that I work under the alias von Durham, after the dictator of Canada, who had written to a young queen Victoria in 1838 that "the Canadian people had neither history nor culture" and that it was better to make it disappear by assimilating it. I refused this suggestion that would have alienated us from our audience from the start. We agreed on the code name of von Chénier, who embodied this liberator full of Prussian military strategies that I prided myself in becoming.

I came to cruelly realize that my conduct gave reason to the famous lord who declared that the French Canadians would buy vengeance and a momentary triumph against the British thanks to "a call to any enemy and by the submission to any yoke."

Hofer clicked his heels and bowed.

"Von Chénier? Perfect! Auf Wiedersehen! One little thing: you do not spit enough when you speak German. Ask Madam: you have to spit at least a meter; otherwise no one will understand you in Berlin. I will be waiting for you there next week, at the Ministry."

He marched out of the room like a military caricature.

I went back to my room heartbroken, and I lay next to Lizbeth who was hiding beneath the covers. I felt as if my whole world was spiraling down. This is the fall the Scriptures talk about, I thought. With difficulty, I stood back up and took Lizbeth's crisped and moist hand. "We will be the strongest. But first, you have to tell me the truth about you and Hofer."

"He means nothing to me anymore."

"But you work for him."

"No. For the Abwehr. I summarize newspaper articles. On steel production. Internal political issues." Our meeting then was not accidental. She had been asked to investigate the separatist movement. I had spent weeks explaining the run of it to her. To save face, I claimed that, already back in Montreal, I had figured it out, and that I was fully aware of it all when I followed her to Kiel.

The halo around the lighthouse was glowing in the thick fog; it was Christmas. It was cold and we had no coal and only sauerkraut to eat. The rivers were frozen. Churchill was saying that he would end the war in Canada if he had to. Hitler answered in the newspapers: "It is probable that only the gentlemen interested in the pursuit of war will exile themselves there. The people, I am afraid, will have to remain in England."

Before leaving for Berlin, we had to pay our last respect to Lizbeth's father. We took the train to the thatch where he had lived next to his temple, near Dortmund. Friedrich, my beloved's brother, welcomed us in the garden where he had taken out his father's furniture and clothes, which he was selling to the neighbors; only a few dared to offer their condolences. He was a tall young man with a bony face and red hair like mine, though the length surely was not in regulation with his navy uniform; his round and dreamy eyes expressed a great determination. On the living room's mantelpiece, between a photograph of the deceased and a bouquet of white lilies, shone the metallic urn the commander of Dachau had sent along with a curt condolence letter. Instead of reading a passage from the Bible, the two orphans recited by heart, in a flat voice, their father's poems, the very ones the SA had burnt in public a few months earlier.

"Light of love! Your golden glory, it also shines for the dead then!" At nightfall, we formed a little procession with a few flocks of readers and pastor colleagues who were walking huddled under a sky reddened by Krupp's highest furnaces, up to a bridge of the Ruhr. The poet's ashes were dispersed over the black river. After the funeral, Friedrich took me aside and told me, as he crushed my hand, "You came to this country for Lizbeth. Not to escape prison nor to make political speeches on the radio. So if you need any help, do not hesitate to call me at the Marine Ministry." Our voices resonated in the house now void of furniture, in front of which Lizbeth was waiting for us, her red scarf flapping in the wind.

"Well," I said clearing my throat in embarrassment, "if you had a tip for a cheap flat in Berlin…"

At first, we did not feel the weight of dictatorship. My first radio performances satisfied my masters and my fees allowed us to rent a small furnished flat on the corner of Joachimstaler and Kurfürstendamm streets, near the Kaiser-Wilhelm cathedral; to the West, the French Infantry was hanging its laundry in the shadow of the Maginot line. The downfall of the British Empire, which I sensed near, justified my wildest pro-independence dreams.

But Lizbeth worried me; she considered the death of her father as murder. Choosing at random in a directory, she addressed anti-Nazi letters to strangers that she would write on a typewriter all day before mailing them in the evening from different mailboxes. Here, censorship was operated from one apartment to the next; neighbors could rat you out to the Gestapo for rebellious remarks made in your own room. But when rage had a hold on her, nothing could make her silent; in a high-pitched voice, that could surely be heard through the walls, she insulted the regime's chiefs: shitheads, scrofulous, impotents, syphilitics. I granted her impunity to Hofer's protection. My doubts were confirmed when he asked me to calm her down. A postmaster had denounced her. He reassured me: these accusations would be returned to the sender. He was, in fact, arrested by the Gestapo two nights later.

I do not wish to go into the details of my performance as a Radio-Berlin speaker. We were broadcasting from Stuttgart. I gave news on the war prisoners: at first, rather well treated; I ironically compared the English officers' menus with the ones for "the little guys back home." Behind the microphone of the Empire Broadcasting Company, in Adolf Hitler Square, I could still meet colleagues from CBS who transmitted, with translations, the Chancellor's speeches. I was spitting fire. Especially after the Dieppe cliff catastrophe: six thousand deaths, the best of the French Canadian youth sent to the slaughter house, photographed in the carcasses of tanks and broken ships. Discontentment and dissonance. The German language was very harsh. My teeth were biting the words, chewing them to say them, breaking on them as on pebbles. In the sink, my blood dripped mixed with saliva; a coughing fit from the depths of the throat like a remote country calling to me on blizzard nights.

Aside from her brother, who had gone back to sea on a torpedo boat, Lizbeth had no family except an aunt in Munich. She worked in Section II at the Abwehr, for General Erwin von Lahousen-Vivremont, at 74 Tirpiz, on the same floor as Admiral Canaris, for whom she seemed to have a boundless admiration.

"He's a fox. But I am so afraid those bastards will end up catching him!"

She told me nothing of her work at the section for sabotage abroad. As it were, we never saw anyone. I would sometimes invite Merry Groves, of the *Chicago Tribune*, but after Pearl Harbor in 1941, such dinners between North Americans became impossible. During the big hockey finals, I snatched a hundred marks by betting against his club, the Chicago Black Hawks and for the Montreal Canadiens.

"You have more judgment for sports than for politics," he said with a wink as he paid me. Hofer also came, with his colleagues from the Berliner Rundfunk. He told atrocious stories about Jews, like this Frau

Liebermann who the Gestapo arrested in her apartment decorated with paintings of her eighty-six-year-old husband Max.

"They carried her out on a stretcher," he said. "She had a tube of Veronal hidden on her and she took it in the ambulance. She was already dead when they arrived at the assembly point of the camp. A very clever old woman. Officially, we burned all her husband's paintings. But in reality, you'll find them in the basement at Gœring's."

Lizbeth had put an end to her musical career, but I insisted that we continue our duets that appeased her while in Montreal. I requisitioned two upright pianos, which, for lack of space, we had to put in different rooms: one in our bedroom and one in the living room, next to the big white porcelain Wilhelm stove. Her fingers and choices betrayed a great sorrow; she cast aside Mozart for Schumann and the latest from Liszt. One day, after I was back from the old royal palace gardens, where Gœbbels had given a reception for the ministry with powdered lackeys holding torches behind tables crumbling under pheasants, I heard her play a heart wrenching piece. She stopped after a few bars but did not come to meet me in the vestibule. I listened carefully to the alarming silence coming from our bedroom, veiled in heavy velvet curtains and furnished with a large German-style bed, so sober with its bolster and its duvet, so different from our Canadian bed with its pillowcases and its colorful quilt.

I repeatedly heard a screeching noise, like the noise of a phone dial and I thought Lizbeth was trying to call Canada, but, as I stepped through the door, I saw our son's mechanical bunny on its wheels covered by grey furry paws.

I dropped it on top of a buffet, upside down so it would wheel its movement in the air, and taking the sobbing Lizbeth in my arms, I swore to her that I would bring back our child. "Don't you understand anything? We have to leave him there. He eats meat every week. He sleeps in his room, far away from those stupid bombers."

"Perhaps, but this separation is killing you."

She wiped her tears on my chest, freed herself from my hold and smiled bravely: "I'll tough it out. The war is almost over anyway, isn't it?"

Through the rare letters that still made it from the German consulate in Portugal, I learned that my family had moved to Quebec. My brother, Captain Perceval, claimed he felt even more cruelly about what he called my treason, since he was part of the intelligence service staff where they openly mocked the cowardice of the "frogs." My son had begun to talk. "In French, surely how you want it to," Perceval specified, temporarily acting as if he were the child's father to avoid any indiscretion that might reveal that Christophe is traitor von Chénier's son.

During his leaves, he brought him to Ancienne-Lorette to see the take off of bombers that would cross the Atlantic after a stop at Gander, Newfoundland, to join the Canadian squadrons that had already begun to attack the German skies.

My brother had married an Acadian from Halifax. With Christophe, she had consoled herself of an infertility she said was only temporary, but no one ever had the chance to verify it as she died on the wreckage of Charlottetown, torpedoed in 1942 off the coast of Matane, one hundred and fifty miles away from its destination, Halifax, where she was to spend two weeks with her family. Christophe was now mourning the death of a substitute mother whose body was never found, while his real one was surviving the bombing of Berlin.

NOTEBOOK FOUR

Behind the microphone of Berlin-Radio, during the winter of the year 1943, I bellowed loud enough to dislocate my jaw. The devil was born from the downfall of reason; the meaning went higher, in a less clear pattern, but even more powerful. I was organizing my spasms. I was spitting the wafer from the tabernacle, how good it was to defy the criminal force that had created us on a night of restlessness.

Attention owners of the Longueuil ammunition factory! Do not bother to paint the roof, you will not need it. The Jean-Étienne Dumont bakery, on the corner of Sainte-Catherine Street and Saint-Laurent Boulevard, will offer a good landmark for the Junkers' bombers. As for the merchants of Saint-Jean Street, in Quebec, who are demanding that the road be widened, rest assured the Stukas will take care of it. Destroy words to better say them.

Unscrew your eyes as to not form any images; soften the lips to pronounce nothing else but ecstasy. Oh! The feeling of the wafer on my palate! This god on your tongue, inducing a sudden and abundant salivation that melts and that we swallow with our eyes closed, attentive to the sacred fall that is formed in the esophagus, flowing all the way to the stomach, ten thousand kilometers lower, because we feel like a mountain, the Himalayas, when God takes a hold of us, and our bodies harbor immense caverns. Give me Patmos, and I will write the apocalypse for you , I will invent exterminator angels for you with faces of mad Jews.

All mighty Father, take me in your arms. Oh! God, my brother must feel so happy when our mother holds him in her arms! But me, no one will console me, not even Nirvana that keeps backing up as I move forward. Hamlet of Quebec is who I am, with an eternal book in his hand and a head full of dark plots doomed to fail.

NOTEBOOK FIVE

During June of 1943, I received an order for a mission signed by Doctor Gœbbels himself, transferring me from the Propaganda Ministry to the Abwehr. They settled to plainly tell me that I was soon to leave for my hometown, for the Quebec that I had almost given up on seeing again as the war dragged on and on. I was flabbergasted.

Catapulted from my comfortable apartment on Kaiserstrasse, where Lizbeth would type my speeches before their broadcast on Radio-Berlin, dispatched very quickly to an Abwehr training camp in Dortmund, I, the intoxicated pencil pusher, the Nelligan of misinformation, escaping the RAF's string of bombs thanks to the scapular given to me by Abbot Dion when I finished my studies at the Séminaire de Québec. I was being subjected to intensive sniper training. An important mission awaited me, judging by the amount of people busying themselves around me, and the high importance given to my movements.

One of the instructors told me that, aside from me, they were able to find, in all the Reich, only one who was reliable and friendly to the

French Canadian cause. So, then they apologized for taking me away from my microphone, but that was when I would learn the purpose of my mission, which would be communicated to me at the very last moment for security measures, I would understand that according to my repeatedly claimed wish, I had been given a date with history.

One night, Lizbeth's brother, Friedrich, asked for me in front of the station without giving his name. He pulled me to a narrow street. He had an arm in a sling and a wound the same color as his bushy hair sticking from under his marine lieutenant cap. After two years in the line of fire, he was now on Tirpiz Quay, under the command of Colonel Baron Wessel von Freytag-Loringhoven, Abwehr Section II chief, thanks to Lizbeth's intervention.

"The baron noticed you during one of the parties at his villa, which explains your mission order. Your boss Hofer is furious and he has complained to Gœbbels. But I did not come for that…" He had to interrupt himself just long enough to cross a square where speakers were blaring a speech from the Chancellor of Stalingrad, here like everywhere else in Deutschland: "Never will the German soldier retreat…" From a deep low-pitch to a high-pitch in the same word, the voice kept screaming over an indifferent crowd.

"You will have a companion on this mission. He will meet you in Quebec. He received orders from Himmler to help with everything, and when it will be time to return, to execute you. Kill him before he acts. And then, come back. You have to come back. Because a traitor's family is also guilty. When they found the authors of the failed assassination attempt, they killed the babies. So Lizbeth, if you were to stay in your Quebec… That is how you like to call your country, is it not? I brought a few documents that might interest you… I am not the only one who thinks the Monster should be killed." He left with an ironic Heil!

I only opened the envelope he had given me once I was back in my room. It was the plans for the integration of Quebec to the Great Reich, elaborated by Hofer in his smoky office on Friedrichstrasse. He had covered the walls with faded maps and fleur-de-lis he gathered during his first stay in Quebec, with Ribbentrop, during the construction of the suspension bridge that a German engineer was able to crumble right in the middle of Saint-Lawrence River due to his erroneous calculations.

After the fall of Poland, defended by hussars on horses as if by many toy soldiers, the Teutonic strategy had become global, and Hofer, jealous of his colleagues' brilliant careers, formerly butchers and now viceroys of Czechoslovakia or Poland, could already see himself as Quebec's gauleiter. He had drawn himself on a poster, ranting from the top of a tribune to a crowd assembled in front of the neo-gothic decor of the Chateau Frontenac. A huge eagle spread its wings over a fleur-de-lis crest.

To Franck, who complained that the Poland he was running did not have enough trees to supply the paper on which he printed his execution orders, Hofer replied that the Quebec forest would allow him to publish the names of the condemned for a thousand years. Knowing to what point Quebec's defenses were ineffective, he had become a very boisterous partisan of a blitz similar to the one that had taken Norway down. A single parachute division, supported a few days later by the landing of a group of panzers would allow him to take over the entirety of Quebec. A hurriedly constituted national government of Quebec, like the ones from Quisling to Oslo, would ensure order on the streets, all while waving to the German troops like liberators from the British yoke. "We would then have a revolver pointed at the industrial United States' temple. Remember, gentlemen, that the fate of the continent was decided in this little town, following the boldness of a divisional general: Wolfe. Let us rewrite history backwards."

My right shoulder was sore from the violent recoil of my weapon during the long hours of training on the firing grounds, but I was still dressed in civilian clothing and I reported to the marine Commander Hans von Gundrich in Kiel. "Ach so, you are von Chénier," he said with a surprising smile in the middle of his red and puffed face due to the long months passed in a steel sarcophagus. "I always listen to your program when we are patrolling the Gulf of the Saint-Lawrence."

"You're Adrien?"

Despite his protests, I knew he was my secret informant, the one who would communicate to me via shortwave the musical program of the different hotels in Gaspésie, with the aim of demoralizing my compatriots by showing that the Axis' spies were everywhere, but also to distract himself, he who had bags under his eyes for less patriotic and more carnal causes than long hours of being awake at the periscope, watching the horizon to find the convoys from the Atlantic.

"Unfortunately, he said, my U-Boat is still not repaired. We won't be leaving for another two weeks."

Von Gundrich, who knew and loved Quebec, invited me to stay in his home. He had worked as an engineer with Hofer, working for von Ribbentrop's firm when the latter had come to build the suspension bridge between the two shores of the Saint-Lawrence. "I had already left your country before the catastrophe, he told me. I hope the Reich and its diplomatic alliances will be more solid than its bridges."

That same evening, when I was trying to reach Lizbeth through a blockade of calls with higher priority than mine, Hofer called to tell me she was seriously threatened with imprisonment for defeatist remarks. But the imminent success of my mission – he thought it to be of the first importance even if he knew nothing of it – would surely give her back her indispensable optimism and would compensate for her father's poor posthumous influence, that homosexual who had suffered from a genetic deformation of character usually virile of the Aryan race.

Von Gundrich burst into my room and invited me on a cruise aboard the Helgoland, the Fürher's yacht where the Great Clown had only been on twice, for propaganda film purposes, showing him smiling and suntanned with the fishermen of the Baltic Sea. "The Helgoland won the New York-Barcelona race in 1937," von Gundrich said nonchalantly, as we left port where the absence of the great battleships, all sunk by now, hit me. "It can always be useful, can't it?" he said with a wink that removed all ambiguity from his word; if the need should arise, he would flee his Fatherland in this small boat.

However, it is the same defeatist, who on a moonless night, refused to hand me the sealed envelope containing my mission order and my fake identity papers before seeing me leave in a submarine. By which means, I do not know, but the Germans had found out that Churchill and Roosevelt, the two masters of the Alliance, were meeting in the capital of their colonial empires, in Quebec, from August 10th to the 15th, to discuss the invasion of the continent. My mission? Eliminate these potentates or, if I failed, find out the location they would choose for the landing.

The Submarine left me in the Chaleurs Bay, in the middle of the night, and then dove, making the sound of a huge sink being emptied. I clumsily paddled to the pier of Paspébiac and immersed my deflated inflatable boat in the lagoon with a Precambrian rock, specific to the region.

At dawn, before leaving the forest and entering New Carlisle where a train left at nine thirty for Quebec, I opened my suitcase only to notice the anachronism committed by Admiral Canaris' spies, as well as the ridiculous Ontarian driver's license, my only identity paper, perfectly imitated by the Nazi forgers if not for the detail that it was in both French and English and that it would have been better to just give me documents completely written in German!

That is why I ended up at the Talbot guesthouse with nothing in my hands, nothing in my pockets, except for a capsule allegedly filled with cyanide that was most likely filled with cod oil.

Winston Churchill dressed like a duchess and wearing a wig, was driving the royal British stagecoach for the high coachman's seat. He was smoking a cigar that his made-up lips smeared with red. In the cabin, we could not see the monarch, but a mound of gold bars that were stacked all the way up to the luggage rack and that made the axels bend. Churchill whipped the two horses that were pulling him towards the Citadelle, Lord Durham's old residence where the new masters of the Western Empire now lived, during the Quebec Conference.

The crash of the hooves echoed on the Saint-Denis gate's arches, and then in the maze of steep alleys that led up to the top of Cap Diamant. Here had ended the story of my people as well as the one of Sleeping Beauty when a traitor delivered the secret of our fortifications to Wolfe's soldiers. Under the equine masks of the draft animals, I suddenly recognized the faces of my father and my grandfather who were neighing in pain under the whip and seemed to be imploring me to free them from their humiliating zoomorphism.

When I awoke, I threw myself under the shower, scalding myself since the cold water faucet turned without results, drank a coffee, diluted to one hundredth of the "Turkish kaffee" I had been accustomed to drinking in Teuton, and then I read in the newspapers that the censors were allowing the announcement of the beginning of the Quebec Conference. In two days, Mrs. Talbot would be requesting payment for the first week. I went to the bank, coming up with an inheritance story in order to change the one-dollar bills that were too big and hadn't been used since 1935 and that the idiots from Abwehr had given me.

Despite the unbelievable failures, the plan of the lords' race seemed to still roll on the bumpy and windy road that History was still following in the part of the country: the night before, I had received the expected visit from our informant, Captain Dansereau of the Quebec Police, the same one who had warned me four years earlier of my imminent arrest. He was ensuring the security of the Quebec Conference, under the supervision of the Royal Mounted Police.

"In two days, Churchill and Roosevelt will be visiting the Plains of Abraham," he told me as he devoured the raw ground meat he had been exclusively feeding on. A little piece of meat stuck on his lower lip, and his frowning forehead made him look like a carnivorous bull. Secretly a Nazi, he commanded an anti-communist and anti-scab squadron. "You won't have a chance to make it out alive," he added with a suspicious glare.

"We'll see. But a good soldier has to obey without criticizing his chiefs," I answered.

He raised his beer and growled: "As you say!"

* * *

In the guesthouse's yard, extenuated, sprawled on a deckchair in my swimming trunks, with the sun licking me with its honey tongue, the branches the wind was swaying, the soft whisper of the chicks; there was no room for desperation in the warm air of this Sunday morning. Mrs. Talbot had left me alone to go to High Mass for the "Saints-Martyrs-Canadiens." I held a cold beer between my naked thighs. The radio was describing a baseball game between the Saint-Sauveur Chevaliers and the Trois-Rivières Royaux.

Germany seemed so far away: its smell of powder, of burnt bodies, of dust lifted by the tanks' tracks, its command cries, its DCA detonations, all that was vanishing with the smell of roses, the soft chiming of a carriage bell going up the hill, the horn of a solitary car, and that bang of a car door coming from the little street, heels in the entrance hall and then on the terrace pavement. My mother was moving towards me, moving in the widow's gown she had worn the day of my father's death.

I did not expect her so quickly after my call. "André?" she asked, stopping as I observed her over the magazine I finally put down. She muffled a cry by biting her right hand gloved in lace. True stare, as with each time sadness was threatening my reason. I rose, to dominate her with my stature, and handed her my beer, which she took and emptied with her head thrown back and a hand on her hip.

"You really came back here in a submarine? That's your style. Are you still angry? You still think that I killed your father by cheating on him."

She weighed the bottle and threw it against the garden wall. "P'tit Christ! Come here!" Arms dangling, I let her hold me tightly against her chest. Her perfume, her hair. "And the ball is... out!" I freed myself from her embrace and turned the radio off.

She said she admires the raging and wrathful energy of my speeches even if they keep repeating the poisoned candy of the ancestral defeats. How could I have joined these obscurantist fascists? It was my father's fault because he brought me up in a circle of hatred. She had thought about it a lot. He would tell me that my people were pitiful. He was ashamed of it, of its way of expressing itself, or rather, of its total lack of expression. These people, like rocks, said nothing. And in that, cornered by logic. I had to differentiate myself from my clan. Condemned to treason.

"I didn't betray my country. I found allies against its enemies."

"What country? Quebec? It's a simple province. You have betrayed all of humanity. Yours. Mine. And not even for thirty deniers." She slapped him with the Abwehr's fake one-dollar note.

"My dearest mom, I whispered. I bet that when I die, you'll arrange for no one to know I ever existed."
"What did you come to do?"

"Kill Churchill and Roosevelt." Cruel, yes. My father had committed suicide due to lack of stories to tell. I was not going to let my rage turn against me.

She burst into laughter. But her eyes were piercing through me. What if I were telling the truth? With me, you could always fear the worst. She took a few steps around the garden, asking me how Lizbeth was doing while I picked a yellow carnation for her. Parents have, behind their mortal faces, the power of ancient gods. My mother: warm and soft perfumes, and a brush smoothing her red hair.

"You're having fun scaring me." It was at that moment that Fagl came into the pension, bending down to pass through the front door and walking down the hall leading to the yard. He was wearing, as agreed upon, the Polish Home aviation uniform, the blue of which suited him better than the usual black of Heydrich's SD. He was German born in the region of Dantzig, so he spoke impeccable Polish. He gave me a military salute and asked me in English where he could find Mrs. Talbot. "I have a lodging coupon," he said while waving a document, at the same time that he questioned me with his eyes he was looking at my mother. I told him to wait in the living room. The lodger would be back from church soon.

"You and that man are pretending not to know each other. Why?" my mother asked once he had left. "He's a killer. One of the most efficient of poor Heydrich, who the Czechs assassinated last year in Prague. Three thousand executions in retaliation. It was him, Fagl, who organized them. He was sent to me because the Germans don't have confidence that I'll accomplish my mission alone."

She had gone white. "Shut up!"
"Oh! There's no chance he'll understand! He does not speak French. That's his weakness. Wait here!"
I went to join Fagl, who was as tense as the springs of a trap ready to snap shut. Short blond curls, pug nose, low forehead, big hands. "Wo ist Roosevelt?" Straight to the point. He was carrying our dismantled assault rifles in his leather bag. Admiral Canaris had split the work between the two of us. Me: Churchill, him: Roosevelt. The security service's reply would only allow us two simultaneous shots, and not consecutive.

I told him I did not know Roosevelt's schedule yet. "Who is that woman?" "No one. A friend of the lodger's. I have to accompany her back home." "Schnell!" I brought him to my room where he collapsed on the bed. His journey from Germany must have been rough.

In the taxi, I did not dare speak to my mother. I asked the driver to take us in front of Chateau Frontenac's terrace. The wind was gentle. Wolfe's fleet had sailed up between Orleans Island and the North Shore. Three thousand cannon balls a day fell on the besieged city. The churches were burning with the wounded on their stretchers.

I had never seen this many people here. The place was crawling with journalists speaking twenty different languages: high-ranking Americans, British and Canadians. Rumor had it that the previous evening, Churchill had ordered a "pig-knuckle stew" and that he almost died from indigestion. The ascetic Roosevelt had been content with eating some Oka cheese.
I saw a few colleagues from Montreal. Completely hidden under my slanted felt hat, in the band of which I had put a press card, and with MacArthur style sunglasses, I walked among them without being

recognized. Officers greeted my mother, who walked beside me without grabbing onto my outstretched arm.

I confessed to her what had been bothering me earlier. "Mom, I was wrong. We can't expect anything from the Germans. Except worse than the English."

"I thank you. It's so nice for your mother to hear that!" she answered me with a smile, a hand on her green wide-rimmed felt hat to stop it from flying off.

"I really don't want to assassinate Churchill. But unless I go back to Berlin with other tangible results, I won't have any other choice but to take action, even if I die trying. Otherwise they'll execute Lizbeth. So I am asking you to talk to Perceval. Ask him to get me a copy of the plans for the European invasion. Real or fake, it doesn't matter. But I want them to have the GQG seal on each page. You hear me?"

Since she continued to walk without speaking, I tucked in my chin and without loosening my lips I yelled: "Death to Churchill! Vive le Québec libre!" A few people turned around, perplexed. But the arrival of two coaches full of American correspondents in front of the hotel's carriage entrance diverted the general attention. Big clouds hid the sun, gusts of wind shook the maples; in fifteen minutes, the weather had cooled down quite a few degrees.

"Free the mayor of Montreal! Down with the conscription!" This time, there was a murmur in the crowd. A few gazes stayed on us, but I remained unshakable, concentrating all my energy in my jaw. Who in this crowd was thinking of Camillien Houde, prisoner of an Ontarian concentration camp in Petawawa? The bald and portly midget had been picked up on the stairs of Montreal's city hall, who, to keep his composure, had begun to sing "Alouette, gentille, alouette," chorus that the anti-conscription mayor still has the leisure to sing during the forced labors, he whom his jailors call the "gros pois" (the "Big Pea").

The moment I filled my lungs with air to yell another slogan, my mother said, "Stop, you win. I'll see what I can do."

I smiled. I swiped the winnings with my only card. The fear of scandal, especially here in front of American journalists who would not let themselves be muzzled by censors: "French Canadian nationalist disturbs Quebec Conference."

"If you can get the minutes of the conference, come to the tribune with a green envelope."

"And the other?"

"Fagl? I'll take care of him." She did not know that Fagl's mission was to leave my body to create dissension among the Allies. A Canadian seems to have killed the Heads of State! A politically stronger act than a murder committed by a German agent.

"I have one last request to ask of you," I added. "I would like to see Christophe." She bit her lower lip in hesitation, and then nodded her head, adding, "He's your son after all. Swear to me you won't involve him in this affair and I'll leave him to you for an hour when Perceval is gone."

* * *

My brother had tried to erase me from Christophe's existence, to turn me into an imaginary character, into a birth certificate mistake. It had become vital that I show myself.

Virginia asked me to wait on the balcony. Through the partially opened curtain I glanced at my son's empty room. There was a painting of a windmill in front of the sea. Christophe must have fallen asleep contemplating it, imagining that stormy waves would not stop it, that a miraculous force moved its arms and that its eyes could pierce the thick fog.

Maybe he was searching for the ship in his dreams- the ship that had carried his fake mother, two years ago. His boat traveled through time and he was waiting for the torpedo that had been launched by the mean Nazi submariner, the explosion of the Charlottetown, and the cries of terror. His ardor doubled, but he always arrived too late- debris, a layer of oil, but no one. Mommy! He screamed while crying, standing up in his boat that rolled dangerously.

Then he would run to the living room. His grandmother was knitting a sweater; Captain Perceval was moving black pins over a map of Europe to show the retreat of the German troops. During these great imaginary maneuvers, he would rail against von Chénier, the traitor of Radio-Berlin that he listened to every Wednesday on the shortwave radio, who would motivate them in French, with a slight Quebec accent, to rebel against the British occupation.

"Christophe, this is your uncle. I'm entrusting you to him," Virginia said as she moved towards the balcony with a four-year-old cherub with golden locks who was hugging her skirt.

"How you look like your mother!" I told my child before gathering him up in my arms and to go back to the taxi that was waiting on the street. I smiled as I put him down in the backseat.

"To the museum!" I ordered the taxi driver. He turned left on Buade Street and he sped up on Grande Allée, which was to the right of the Parliament. He turned sharply to the left on a paved road that led to the Plains of Abraham, rather deserted in the middle of the afternoon, and parked in front of the Doric colonnade.

On August 10th 1943, my son was following me in the museum, through the sun-filled rooms, where stuffed bears bared their teeth and claws over a wax Algonquin kneeling in the dusty air of the display case. We went up the marble staircase, up to the last floor. I waited to be alone with him and then, through a hidden door; I reached the flat and tar-covered pebble roof. From there, the sight could go from the purple dales of the Laurentian Chain to the north, to the Chateau Frontenac, whose dungeon resembled the rear forecastle of a galleon, the Cap Diamant, pointing towards the estuary, to the opposite shore of the Saint-Lawrence, thin black and steep stripe between the pure sky and the sparkling river. Christophe was squeezing my hand.

"You see that city with the walls? It's cold, cold even in summer. We have been freezing and dying there for two centuries. At school, you will be told that it is our homeland. But it is nothing. A homeland is a father speaking in his child's ear. You don't have a father anymore, it seems, and I have lost my son. Do you know how they took our country away?"

At the far end of the plain, which stretched over two kilometers, I pointed to an indentation in the trees that opened on Anse-aux-Foulons, the spot where Wolfe's army landed in 1759. The sheer cliff dove into the Saint-Lawrence that the French cannons of the time were still aiming at.

Here, the traitor Vignol had let the Scottish battalions climb up; they had deployed behind their delicate and red headed general, absolutely determined to destroy New France. Enraged by the mocking sound of bagpipes, Montcalm had ordered his troops to leave the ramparts. They marched in a disorderly fashion, with cries to give themselves courage. The English, on the other hand, were only counting on their silent discipline and the constant barrage of their infantry squares.

"We prefer to forget," I told my son, "but the winners, they remember. In a few days, they'll visit the Wolfe column, erected to their past glory."

I heard the whipping flags that surrounded the stage down below, where Churchill and Roosevelt would receive the salute from the Citadelle's guard and would continue to discuss their plans to invade Europe, a subject they had not agreed upon by the beginning of August. From my observation point, it was about half a kilometer, which the bullets from my Mauser equipped with a telescopic lens could easily cross. I was already imagining Churchill's silhouette. If my mother did not bring the documents, von Chénier would have reason over Lord Durham, proving we had a history that could violently collide with that of the world. I brought Christophe back at four on the dot, just as I had promised Virginia.

The same evening, Dansereau called me to give me the time of the official visit of the next day's visit to the Plains. Fagl and I left the Talbot guesthouse to set ourselves up on the museum's roof. The visitors were expected the next day at ten in the morning. The area would not be sealed off before dawn. I had already seen Fagl in action. He was a surprising beast of speed and ruse. I assembled my Mauser. We had a night of gin and fusing stars, of terror and eve. He showed me a photograph of his fiancée: Bavarian suspenders over an ample nude chest. He pissed in the middle of the roof in an air duct.

It was not him who killed, but rather it was a dog that bit his gut and forced him to act. He was calming the beast; he was stroking it. With a weapon of this quality, he only had to rub the trigger with his index. Fagl cried as he thought about his victim. "Oh my god, what suffering factories pour down here," he said as he hit his stomach, he shook as if racked by an epileptic fit. He was searching for peace in final spasms of the ones he killed.

As I kept watch, my blanket wrapped around my shoulders as he slept a few hours. One bullet makes a difference in history. I would still be hated in a thousand years.

There was already a lot of activity around the stage. A grenadier brass band was rehearsing God Save the King. A few policemen were setting up fences in front of the bystanders drawn in by the preparations that remained a mystery to them as censors forbade the newspapers from reporting Churchill and Roosevelt's movements.

"They will be here soon," said Fagl. A long line of cars was approaching with honking, preceded by several Jeeps. The passers-by stopped, some waved their tricolor flags, or the Union Jack. We lay flat on our stomachs, hidden behind the Doric pediment. The cars stopped and he came out. My victim. Churchill. Never saw so much ferocity on a face before. Apoplectic. Consumed by rage. Coming from the depths of history. Conqueror, builder of empires. The other, Roosevelt, dull. His shoulders drooped under his black tweed cape.

They both sat in deep padded sofas, which contrasted with the folding chairs reserved for the other guests. We were waiting for the coming and going around the stage to stop so that we could shoot. My mother was there. I took aim with my rifle. "On the first strike of the cymbal," Fagl said, pointing to the brass band. At the same moment, my mother bent down and took a green envelope out of her handbag which she nonchalantly fanned herself with.

I would get what I wanted: numbered documents sporting the authentic seal of the Head of State of the Empire. And by the time the codes of this outdated document were broken, the war would most likely be over. The grenadier smashed his cymbals; I shot a bullet in Fagl's head. Already muffled by the silencer, the shot went undetected. The blood and brains mingled with the roof's gravel. I heard the grateful applause of three thousand tortured Czechs. I crawled to the other end of the roof facing the river, and wrapped myself once again in the blanket that had kept me warm the previous night, because despite the sun, my teeth were still chattering. I would have to wait at least an hour before I could leave the museum.

The train dropped me off in New Carlisle. I had put on Fagl's Polish uniform. I had amused myself by answering the other passengers' questions in a terrible French, while humming mazurkas and demanding vodka from the conductor. An American family on holiday found me to be particularly "touching," especially the eldest of the two daughters who tormented me so that I would recite poems in Polish to her.

I complied by reciting some verses by Schiller, which sounded to her like terrible Warsaw gibberish. "Your poor country," she said as we rode on in their rental car. I was wary of the silent and sullen father, who had stuffed his hunting rifles and his camping gear between our legs on the back seat, so I exaggerated my drunkenness.

Two kilometers before arriving in Paspébiac, he suddenly braked and left me in the middle of the deserted road, swearing that I was a bloody French Canadian as true as he was born in Krakow. He said that he would report me to the military police as soon as they got to Percé. He spit in my direction. "You're all fucking deserters!" he yelled before starting the car. Instead of following the road, I went straight through the fields towards the coast, chewing on maple leaves I tore off along on the way and that had the same taste as my feeble fate; the moose bellowed as if to warn each other of the coming of the Polish hunters from Pittsburgh.

The Chaleurs Bay glittered under the lighthouse's rotating beam. The night usually helped the Sons of liberty. In its dragon skin, I found rest. I arrived at the cottage my father had built in 1932 at the tip of Paspébiac.

I broke the door down with one strike of my heel. Thankfully, tourists were rare during August of 1943; our usual neighbors had not come that year nor could they attest to the boarded up windows. I ate Franco-American macaroni and canned beans in lard, because I did not dare cook anything should the smoke signal my presence. I waited in the smell of rotten wood, freezing, listening to the rain fall on the tin roof, reading old newspaper, the wet pages of which fell apart in my hands.

The hell of always leaving, of no longer having a country, and destroying the one you had just begun to build. Where is my Jerusalem? In my mind, I saw Fagl's face exploding from the inside, from the dum-dum bullet shot. My mother promised me that she would meet me here, where I was to meet with von Gundrich.

An engine was getting closer, muffled as it went uphill and high-pitched when going down. I waited on the porch, the Mauser on my knees, convinced that I would see the RCMP's red tunics. But it was Perceval's Buick that appeared around the curb. The wind from the speed ruffled my son's hair; he had his head out the window. My mother greeted me with a wave. I hid my weapon as I walked over to greet them. Christophe ran up the path: "Uncle! We came to surprise you."

My mother ran her hand in my four-day-old beard. Perceval shrugged off his khaki vest, rolled his sleeves and opened the trunk. "André! Come help me carry the supplies! No, Christophe, don't touch that weapon!" My son took his hand off the Mauser. I shrugged. "It wasn't loaded." As he handed me a heavy box of supplies, he whispered: "It was the other day though... The official press release says that the forces of order shot a Nazi agent; another one is on the run. Who could contradict us? Be careful with the eggs..."

My mother opened the shutters. We could hear the puff-puff of a fisherman's barge as he collected his lobster traps near the reef. My son was collecting pinecones and was bringing them back to me, laughing. I drew a spiral on an empty toilet paper roll that I stuck in a potato that was turning placed directly on the stove's hotplate. Christophe clapped his hand before the never-ending rotation of the circular propeller, just as I had done with my father.

I was hungry and I devoured the steak Perceval had been able to get us despite the rationing. To be happy, you just need to be with the ones you love, to be with the flesh of your flesh, beautiful, smiling, curious and breathless. This moment happened, not even spoiled by the desire to prolong it. After the meal, my son went to bed with my mother in the bedroom; I went to chop wood in front of the bay with Perceval. "I brought what you had asked Virginia," he told me. "I caught her just as she was taking the documents out of my briefcase. She told me about you and Lizbeth. I was all right with it. We're all traitors now."

My axe split the log Perceval was holding. He wiped off a spider web that had gotten stuck to his face when he was in the shed.

"I'm telling you a secret; Virginia doesn't know about it. I don't think I'll see the end of the war," he said. I'm dying of cancer. And the landing isn't for this year."

"Perceval... I'm sorry." In truth, that news saddened me deeply. Even though everything – language, religion, and politics – should have made my half-brother an enemy, he was, along with Friedrich, my only true friend.

"How is Lizbeth?" he asked. "Rotten story. We record all your speeches in our archives. You're on our most wanted criminals list. You'll never be able to come back. But what if the traitor became a double agent, a hero after the war, decorated by Her Majesty?"

"Especially not that! I will never fight against the English, but against the Nazis… maybe! And you'll have to keep the secret until the end, because there's a traitor among your staff."

"Precisely, we'd like to know how the Germans found out about Churchill's trip to Quebec. It was a formidably well-guarded secret."

We climbed the hill that was overlooking the ocean. With their necks squeezed between their wings, the seagulls were watching us with suspicion; on the anvil of the horizon, sparks glittered under the red sun. He took a green envelope out of his thick jacket. "Here's the plan the SHAEFF adopted for the invasion of the continent. There's the code to use to transfer the information to me via Berlin-Radio. No one knows about my offer. If you accept, I'll remain the only one to know. I'll say I stumbled on the code by chance, but that I don't know the true identity of our air-wave informant."

Thunder rumbled. Rain began to fall. Then a ray of sunshine lit up the rock. Quickly, a blue circle spread in the sky, above the cliffs carved in the backlight, on top of which the fog frayed; the mountains were still huddled beneath the motionless clouds, and at the entrance of the bay, two rainbows were rising over the Atlantic, like the pillars of an invisible temple.

"Leave me alone with Christophe. I'll give you an answer when you come back."

I walked them to the car. I took my mother in my arms one last time. I went for a walk in the forest with Christophe. We saw a blue chick fallen from its nest, dragging its broken wings on the ground. It is the noblest of pity to finish off animals that are suffering. But I did not have the courage to do so. I placed it on a cushion in the living room and gave it dry milk and breadcrumbs that it could peck at from the palm of our hands.

The lichen covered the limbed out pine tress on the side of the rocky beach. The still swelled up sea was crashing against the rocks. On a dead tree, a thrush was puffing itself in shivers; the wet grass had already soaked my shoes. The sun's refractions in the branches threw nets between the trees. A rabbit sitting still turned its ears towards us. I stopped for a long while, not wanting to scare off the animal, nor did I want to scare off the moment of peace that I could savor for the first time since I had left Quebec.

I told Christophe the story of the corsair who, surrounded by the British navy, had set rafts on fire around his boat to make them believe, at night, that he also had a large fleet. "Do you want to do the same thing he did? Come!"

On the beach, we lit up the four woodpiles I had set up as agreed upon with von Gundrich: two at each end of the creek. Then, we sat on a tree trunk as I continued my stories. In my satchel, I had put Perceval's documents as well as some of Christophe's things for the trip. With the sky covered, I had the impression of looking out onto nothingness. I suddenly heard the swashing of oars and the rhythmic cries of the rowers: "Eins, eins, eins, zwei, drei!" I kneeled in front of Christopher and told him in German: "Listen, Ich bin dein Vater. And no matter what anyone tells you, I did not betray my country." I climbed the dune in a hurry and hid the child behind a bush: "Don't move," I told him in French. "Don't speak. I don't want you to meet my friends. I'll come and get you soon. You'll tell Perceval I agree."

As I was going back towards the beach, the inflatable raft emerged in the night. I disappeared with the feeling that I was losing my son forever. As we hurried back to the U-Boat 451, I tightened my grip of the documents Perceval had left me.

Rocked from one side to the other in the steel coffin nailed to the bunk where the smell of gasoline, farts, urine and sauerkraut were making me nauseous, with Commander von Gundrich that had cabled Berlin to give them the result of my mission, I listened to the submarine's sonar play cat and mouse with the destroyers of the Atlantic fleet, the U-Boat 451 having been given strict orders to avoid all contact with the enemy and to rush to Kiel, to hand me over, me and my precious documents, into the hands of the Fourth section of the Abwehr.

Gundrich claimed I would get a hero's welcome; I was not so sure of that. My mission had failed, Fagl was dead and I placed a feeble hope for salvation in the secret false documents I was bringing back. I had left my four-year-old son behind, on a deserted beach on the Chaleurs bay, whispering a secret to him that he would soon forget once in his grandmother's arms, who would tell him it was all just a nightmare. I had set off again, far from the welcoming and peaceful shores, where I could have lived for thirty years in solitude, looking at myself, like Narcissus, during the summer in the rivers full of agile salmon, during the winter on the ice of the arctic lakes where branches gnarled broken by the wind emerging like shriveled up fingers from the other side of the mirror; I could have transmitted all my knowledge and my vision of the world to a new generation of hopeless people, but I was leaving on my sub-aquatic steed toward a crumbling Europe, towards Germany that was tiring itself in the Ukrainian steppes. I wanted to heal my inner plague so as to not pass it on to my son. And I was returning to that country where it reached endemic proportions, where gigantic factories were taking millions of humans apart on a production line. Because I understood the hate and I was so horridly close to it, I preferred to abandon Christophe. Despite my immense need to love him, I did not know how to talk to him, how to tame him; like my father with me, I only knew how to bring him to a lunar crater where we would disassemble bodies to understand how they work. Because I only dreamt of death and of perfection, I was a fascist deep down, even if at this moment I was about to work for the Allies.

I could only return to Germany, to explain myself in this vortex of pain and cataleptic jigs. But if I could break this curse, I would return to Quebec to hold my son against my chest again, and Lizbeth would come with me. She would follow me like the lost half of myself.

I will first recount my return to the capital, to this Berlin that was no longer at sea level, despite the cartographers' statements, but that was sinking into an abyss, the walls of which were made from the Westphalia Plains, from where we watched the flying fortresses lay, launching eggs from their metal hulls that would hatch into the subway tunnels and shelters as the DCA searched these crisp and aerial waters, like the numb and powerless fingers of a drowning man trying to reach the surface. Never-ending knit of railway tracks that were pulsating beneath the first-class wagon, Hitlerian salute from the needles that spread us out on each side of the covered convoy, heavily loaded with panzers, rolling eastbound, huge horizon where the last wheat fields of Ukraine burned. I held the briefcase tightly to my chest, with red velvet seats on both sides of the two Abwehr officers, high-collared and crested caps like the tufts of an owl, and I was sure, from their frigid looks and their barked orders, that my destination was the incinerator.

From Wilhemkœnig Station, an armored Mercedes brought us to Admiral Canaris' office, Tirpiz Quay. My boss for this mission smiled as he looked over the documents and declared, "Fakes, skillfully made! But if the English are trying to fool us, they have their reasons, just like you must, if you work for them. And we, by discovering those hidden motives, we will learn as much as if we had the authentic documents. This deduction game, I am the only one interested in it. I will transmit these invasion-plan documents to the SII, with your condolences and mine for Fagl's death, a close friend of Heydrich's. It is a pity he went and pushed his insolence to the point of driving a convertible through a town where he had thousands executed. The people of Prague decidedly have no gratitude. Congratulations and… Heil!"

Poor Canaris, who'd had his whistle cut with piano wires a week earlier. Refusing to confess until the end, losing his torturers in the logical labyrinth of his replies, but lost through the discovery of his hidden notebooks, though he had them poured into a safe under his safe, but that not even he could resist filling up, as if the means of this solitary and silent speech turned out to be indispensable for the survival of the soul.

In 1943 though, Canaris had enough weight to save my life and change, if he so judged it, a mission that had ended up a fiasco into a glorious operation of his own service, the Abwehr. Thanks to his protection, which was highly self-motivated since he himself would have been compromised with a failure, I was able to escape a tight interrogation from the Gestapo.

I walked to the Propaganda Ministry to report back to Hofer from whom I had temporarily been detached for this expedition, which I now saw as completely conceived by the Intelligence Service from beginning to end. The team of Radio-Berlin had prepared a triumphant welcoming for me. Several suspected that this alleged mission was, in reality, an excuse to send me to my death.

They did not really know what exploits I had accomplished in America, and I could not tell them the juicy details that the Admiral had classified as "sehr geheim," but the maple syrup and the newspapers I brought back were enough to convince them I had indeed seen Canada again.

Jacques-Edgar Paradis stayed behind his desk in the writing room and grew darker as I gave news from over there.

"Two feet in the river with a bag of fries and a bottle of Coke, I watched the boats go by. It was beautiful!"

"Did you eat hamburgers? Yes? Lucky bastard!"

The only other Quebecer in Berlin with me, he had lost his access to the microphone when he announced, on July 28, 1942, that the Reichwehr had just freed all of the Canadian prisoners captured in Dieppe from the Saint-Denis camp, mistaking his wishful thinking for reality. Since that incident that had put an end to the live broadcast and forced the Paris-Canada section of Radio-Berlin to emit an erratum, poor Paradis recited prayers in his office where he was sure the Gestapo would come and get him.

"How are my parents?" he asked me nervously as he twisted his armband with the swastika under a fleur-de-lis. I did not know. " Heartless!" and he left, swallowing a sob. I was never to see him again.

I approached the studio's glass wall. The couple greeted me: Suzanne-Fernand Le Bailly and Paul Dagenais; two old French residents from Montreal sent to Berlin by the Pétain government. A red light went on; the recording was starting. After the Alouette song, which served as an indicator, the Vichyssois expressed their profound sadness as true Frenchmen that the French Canadians were used as cannon fodder for the Anglo-American Empire, not only in Dieppe, but also in North Africa and Sicily, as the obituaries testified, and which they took upon themselves to read to the people. Reminding them that the Führer had offered independence to Quebec, as well as a financial agreement with the Great Reich, they invited along with that gesture, their sound-effects engineer to imitate the sound of bubbling champagne mixed with Seltzer water, to celebrate the results of a Gallup survey done in secret for the federal government, so they said.

"The Musical Candy Box," which they hosted twice a week, during which they played songs from Chevalier and Trenet, reached thirty percent of Quebecers, fifty percent in the most remote regions highly equipped with shortwave radios. But it was I, the virulent von Chénier, who obtained the highest ratings, because I continued with our pamphleteer tradition, from Arthur Buies to Jules Fournier, ensuring that the truth was known by all, despite the repressions of British censors.

That being said, Suzanne-Fernand greeted me with a wink, then putting on a record, she skipped towards me to kiss me and asked if I had heard them from over there. "The Canadians are threatening to scramble our radio waves. What lack of fair play!" she said with a middle-aged girlish pout.

She found that dear Hofer was a little sad as of late. "After having had a taste of the Russian winter, the generals don't really want to test the Quebec blizzards. Our future gauleiter is seeing his future empire slipping away from him. But your returning with good news is sure to cheer him up." She told me to run to him at his suburban villa where he was healing a bad cold. I saw her partner from the corner of my eye reprimand her as if she had just made a faux pas.

She stopped sharply and said, "What was I thinking? Before that, you wanted to kiss your charming Lizbeth. Excuse me, I have to get back on." Suzanne-Fernand having changed her mind so quickly raised a few suspicions that I did not want to explain clearly. I went down to the Ministry underground garage where I had left my car for safe keeping in the hands of the janitor in exchange for some Dutch gin. I removed the tarp that covered the engine and gave it a kick-start full of rage. Instead of heading towards Tempelhof, where our modest cottage was, I went up Unter den Linden, covered at the time with chestnuts and dead leaves, to the east, towards the posh Spandau where Hofer had received me on several occasions the previous summer.

As I sped up, I was trying to re-learn the excesses of the now, the percussion that follows each breath, the creation of the ordinary universe with each wink, the desert of entrails, the ecstasy that comes when you stop thinking, the solid links of dreams, the search for a unique voice, the one that is God's. I also noticed that nothing changes; there is no other universe, perhaps only a way to place the world in emptiness. I was a turtle among snakes. I was following the Speer; roofless, I squeezed my BMW through the freezing September rain between the double-decker buses that were changing their course according to the bomb holes, the Mercedes of the Nazi dignitaries, the wounded that flowed back from the east, the mounds of garbage where bottle shards glittered.

At the end of the acceleration, I found stupefaction. It is a matter of rhythm, I told myself. I braked in front of Hofer's villa. It was a whimsical construction, rococo, all of gables and half-timber, with a great garden where tons of bird houses rose on poles, painted like the signs of barbershops, with red and with spirals. His rank as gauleiter of Quebec was still too imaginary to warrant him a military guard, so there were no obstacles as I walked up to the massive double door, surmounted with a fleur-de-lis bas-relief. A chain with an ivory handle activated the doorbell that played "Vive la Canadienne."

The master of the domain opened the door; he was dressed in a red plaid shirt, his feet encased in lumberjack boots. Shocked for a moment, he grabbed me heartily by the shoulders, and shook me vigorously, as if to confirm my physical presence. "Von Chénier! You survived! You came back! The essence Quebec heroes are made of!" His breath stank of Schnapps. I entered the hall. Lizbeth appeared in the door that led to the living room where logs were joyfully burning in front of a grizzly skin lying under the stone-faced gaze of a moose head. "You know of my passion for photography? Lizbeth accepted to take part in a session."

She resembled the character of a Zurbaran painting. A soft air, resigned, her blond hair falling on a purple negligee out of which came puffy white sleeves, the saint offered her cut breasts on a platter, like two perfectly cone-shaped ice cubes drenched in the red sauce of her own blood. As she fixed her outfit, her arm on the doorframe, her hair in a tangle, her eyes red and puffy from lack of sleep, I saw that her thighs were sporting marks from a crop.

I wanted to hold her in my arms, but she beat my chest while calling me a Dummkopf, scolding me for having come back, and when I told her that if I had not she would have been executed, she screamed that she would have preferred to be dead, that I had only prolonged the torture.

I was trying to spot the shadow of an emotion on Hofer's face, but only the devil could decipher his reptilian soul. "Do not look at me like that! Lizbeth is still my legitimate wife, nein? Actually, you could not marry her even if I divorced her. The law protects our Aryan racial capital from your Iroquois genes." He imitated the cries of savages while tapping his mouth. "You are right on time, dear friend. I was waiting for you to celebrate a burial. Come!" He pushed me towards the villa's garden.

"One moment!" I turned to Lizbeth: "Are you putting your coat on?" I said while kissing her. She tilted her head and blew me a kiss as I threw over her shoulders the loden coat a servant had brought with an insulting smile. We went out. A coffin of badly squared-off boards rested on two trestles. "Do you know what it holds?" Hofer declared. In a dramatic gesture he opened the lid: "Quebec!" I saw books, posters, flags, all marked with fleur-de-lis. "A country can only be born in blood. And you did not want to kill! Alone, Fagl would have succeeded. You made him fail. Without the protection given to you by that imbecile Canaris, I would have quickly known what happened. Even the Gestapo cannot interrogate you about your mission… With Churchill killed, I had a squadron of parachutes leaving from Oslo this morning and heading for Quebec after a stop in Reykjavik. Now they will be leaving for Stalingrad. Burn, Quebec!"

He threw a match on the logs he had staked underneath the coffin. The works of Groulx, Dostaler O'Leary, Wilfrid Morin began to burn as Hofer poured Schnapps on them. I really wanted to hit him, but that would have condemned me to death. Just like Lizbeth sitting on the saddle behind me, while the other continued his acting and was telling me to "party with her" all nightlong; he would wait until morning for me to make my report.

I turned the gas levers to the max. The world is a collection of facts, not things. The pain in my abdomen made me want to rip myself out of my body.

My acts of kindness became violent. While my brain was pouring its toxic substances on my insides, I preferred to roll. I found a temporary peace on the motorcycle, my arms shaking from the handlebars, the vibrations of the engine between my thighs, the heels of my boots wedged on the footrest. At a low altitude, just over a viaduct where a Wehrmacht convoy had been blown up, a Mosquito was passing, pointing like the finger of God towards the Tiergarten's forest where I wanted to be alone with Lizbeth.

She tightened her hold around my waist and caressed me. Let this delirium be, as long as it remained purely physical, in the base of the body's baroque architecture. To hurt, to split, to lose oneself in the illusion, to slow the descent of the scavengers down on our conscience. Free Quebec of all the Hofers; let sense gush out like blood. The glow from a passing convoy's headlights crossed the frozen cosmos of my brain. On the boulevard, the caress created a maelstrom. I stopped photographing the moment. I accelerated swiftly: the speed clustered the light posts in the centerline into a green wall, the memories of the Gold of Rhine gave me Wagnerian goose bumps on the back of my neck. The moon in its last crescent was baiting the predatory black sky that would gobble us all.

I was brooding over what everyone knew: I was not self-sufficient. Solitude and worry drove me insane. I needed to find allies, companions, a nation. I needed to drink and destroy myself; another existence became brutal. I had thought I would be able to look at it coldly, philosophically. What a terrible mistake! Objectivity killed. I had to commit excesses. They were committing them against me all the time. I am happy; I yelled to the cover, the cylinder shaped demons that were backfiring against my ear, and behind their rough voices. I found silence.

I was trying to stand there, in the past, before everything was spoiled. But to make Germany disappear, that was impossible. I was touching it, smelling it, rubbing my nose, my intestines, my eyes, my ideas in it, she came in and out, cuddling against me, just like Lizbeth, whose cheek I could still feel against my shoulder blades.

Grossman Street. The sky jagged by the linden trees. I wanted to kneel down and adore it. How far could this darkness carry us? I went into the Tiergarten on a deserted path, whirring, turned into a slough by the rain. I was looking for the high point of absence to recover from existing in the same universe as Hofer. I felt sucked in by the peak of this trail cluttered with tree trunks. It was then the lights of the BMW lit up a field of grass that was waiting for us like a nest on the side of the path.

"I want to meet your brother! Tell him I have a coded antenna for America and that I'm willing to transmit his group's information," I whispered in her ear, after I had recounted my journey and more importantly, after having described all of our son's words and actions.

NOTEBOOK SIX

It's the End of the world, with the blood of Berlin flowing out in great gushes through the bomb holes; great victories followed by three years of defeat. This story will be manipulated, swallowed and regurgitated by Gœbbels' impeccable propaganda machine, or rather by his successor, since the clubfoot will soon burn along with his wife and his children.

I love the shapeless larvae of this war, the millions of bodies that I created that are now my only possession, the one that no enemy will ever be able to take away from me, and with ease that brings bliss and trance. I am hiding at the end of the bunker. I would need a periscope like in the trenches in 14. I don't dare stick my nose outside because of the one-ton bombs that fall from the holds of the flying fortresses. There's a risk it would slow me down. So, I'm counting on my messengers, who bring false news because I don't want to hear the real news anymore and if I do, I threaten them with death.

Christmas. I feel good, but my right hand is shaking more and more. (The situation in Hungary!) For the last two days, feeling of uneasiness and gassiness, a consequence of pea soup. The larynx is perfectly healed, despite the fact that I still have the feeling there is a slight irritation.

I slept in the bunker because the enemy planes were disturbing my sleep. What can be done to stop my right hand from shaking? I refuse sedatives, because they would slow down my mental process and that would be catastrophic considering my current responsibilities.

I become a fiction, I invent myself to the degree of my fear, and from Moscow to Tangier, from the Ridge to Norway, my fear is immense! We had to stop the ventilation in the bunker because it was sucking in the smells of sulfur from the outside, from the bombs, the dust of Berlin; the Berliners charred behind their pieces of artillery, like my brother-in-law, Fegelein who was executed for having tried to escape.

I am hardening, like granite: the flesh is dead. I go to the kitchen to retrieve a remaining piece of cake, and I prepare to fulfill my ultimate promise: "At the moment of supreme danger, I will disappear."

"So, from a literary point of view, what do you think?" Hofer asked me as I finished deciphering the shaky spidery scrawl that he had given me to read that night.

Despite a mine launched by parachute that had destroyed the Empire Broadcasting Company's south wing, we were still broadcasting, but from our underground studio. And we had our service meetings in the neighboring bars. The camera that was used to microfilm still worked and Hofer brought me new documents from the Führerbunker to photograph everyday.

"Adversity gives great men wings," I answered.

"I admit I feel honored by the mission I was given," Hofer said, teary eyed. "Taking to Canada the Führer's lyrical expression and ensuring its publication later, when the time is right. This noble task fell upon Gœbbels but he decided to commit suicide… What an idiot! As for the Führer, he had a tunnel dug beneath the bunker, an escape route where he could wait as the events unravel. As for me, I prefer to disappear."

He burst into a booming laughter. The Helgoland was waiting for us in Kiel, well hidden from the bombs in the fortified U-Boat harbor. It was von Gundrich himself who was supposed to take us to the freedom and safety of my coveted Quebec. I repositioned myself on the velvet seat. I stretched. I was looking for a rhythm that would make me sleep in the artillery's rumble. Everyday, in the Adlon Hotel's underground bar, next to the Brandenburg Gate, with the diplomats of neutral countries, Hofer and I would write even wilder and more frenzied propaganda as the Russians were getting closer. We asked everyone to write a note on a piece of paper, to roll it tightly and then to slip it in the belly dancer's garments.

She went around the room and came back to our table, swaying her hips, and carrying the primary substance of the next release destined to cheer up the troops and signed by Gœbbles. A cash register clinked at the back of the bar. We were waiting for the words to die out, mouth wide open, as if we were fishing with dynamite. There would not be one left alive. We would kill them all with the little notes we read out loud. The barman was playing Glen Miller on the gramophone. The trumpet was "debaptizing" the universe since its creation; exterminating the rats from the tabernacles. Ah! Lohengrin and Walhalla! The music was destroying us; nothing would beat the last shock in its harmonic vagina, if not for its wicked return. Nietzsche was right: every pleasure has a thirst for deep, deep eternity. The music was pushing us even further toward the end. A tall SS was standing up and slapping a French prostitute, a Kokotte. The bottles on the bar were clinking against each other. The gin added vinegar to my ulcers.

Hofer told me that some technicians were going to move the camera to the Führerbunker so I could continue my archiving work until the very last moment.

"Hang in there, mein Freund. We will soon be in Gaspésie."

* * *

We were camping in the basement of our villa, Lizbeth and I. A candle was molding the shadows in conniving and moving arches. Our breaths became entwined. The world above us is exploding, meine Liebe. Her breasts tensed under the silk, she was eating a potato as she read my palm.

"It seems you will meet a great love, I think!" Lizbeth said with a sad smile, soon to be stuffed in the museum of eternity. We would all go through, and quickly. No matter how much we stuck our chests out, in the pit and curtain! No problem.

I did not want her to know that the Gestapo had seized my latest recording. For what purpose other than to decipher the code I was using during my transmissions to Perceval? Who had ratted me out? They would come to arrest me within the next few hours. And I did not want Lizbeth to be around at that moment.

"Look at what my brother Friedrich gave me!" She took a grenade out of the chest drawer. She primed the grenade and looked me right in the eyes. Nothing. The detonator did not work. It took us a few minutes to settle down from our fit of laughter.

I climbed up to the very last stair that led to the villa's garden. "Go see your brother, I told her. He has to be told about the tunnel under the bunker. They have to blow it up. No one must escape."

96

She was sobbing. I rested my forehead against the wall. She passed behind me and brushed my dangling right hand. "Auf Wiedersehen!" she said. I did not answer. She was walking away in the devastated garden, skipping between the beams and the slate tiles that had fallen off the roof. I had always believed her face would be that of my death.

I went back in. An immense outcry brushed against my skin. Rent your own name, prostrate yourself before it. Know that the mirror shows only a minute part of your face. Deprived of purpose, I was becoming a monster. I couldn't breathe without my love. Do not deceive me, oh my torturers! It was dawn. I was waiting for you. I wanted you to dispossess me. I wanted you to make me into a man without a history.

The sky was becoming overcast with planes, the windows were shaking, squares were being pulverized and blocking the sun, followed by a moment of peace. The undisturbed chirping of sparrows. Brakes cringed. Two Gestapo policemen in civilian clothes slammed the doors of a black sedan in front of our villa. Where were they still finding gas? I went to meet them. "Where is your wife?" I shrugged. They pushed me on the backseat like a lifeless body.

We drove through the ruins, two motorcycles escorting us and a half-track behind us, following a complicated trajectory, bumpy, with sudden stops that hurt me since I could not protect my face with my hands that were shackled behind my back. My lips bleeding, I was trying to catch my breath as a soldier left on his BMW in reconnaissance to figure out how to go around a bomb whole.

On the corner of Kurfürstendamm and Berlin Allee, hanging from light posts, three Hitlerian youths were oscillating from the end of their ropes; the moon lit the face of one of the teenagers. I recognized the son of our neighbors who had participated in the ski descent at the Tiergarten: thousands of young people forming a swastika with torches to bait the allied pilots. Now his tongue was hanging out and he had a sign around his neck: I am a coward.

The car started up again; I tried to hold on between my two jailors who were both holding onto the car door handles. The rubble unfolded, attracting in their empty unknown spaces the powerful winds from Ukraine, Byelorussia, Finland, on the heels of the German army, and they were digging grooves in the ash of department stores, the proud marble villas, the opera houses, the cathedrals. Crematory nightmare. At the end of Unter den Linden, even more extensive than the Champs-Élysées, the angel of victory, miraculously intact, was spreading its golden wings in front of the Brandenburg Gate.

We are but love that passes or that does not pass. Jaws opened in stupefaction, I did not fear death anymore. I did not have a grip on anything. Wall sections were looking at us with their hollowed out windows. The sirens were spreading their sound blanket beneath the clouds that the DCA spotlights' luminous fingers were blindly searching for, as if frantically trying to pick all the metal ticks that were proliferating out of it.

I was being dragged through a mountain of rubble. Not to a firing squad, like I feared. To my great surprise, I found myself in a still intact vault. A torturer in a white smock sculpted my teeth, without anesthetic, with a dentist's drill plugged into an emergency generator. He would sometimes stop to look at x-rays hanging from a piano wire that was hung across the room by two hooks. My head squeezed into the clamp that was holding my mouth opened, I lost consciousness several times.

Revealing Lizbeth's whereabouts seemed to be the only way to end the torture. I became delirious. I was going down a staircase, which was lit from below by a green glow, to an underground lake of crystal clear water, with a fine sandy beach and, in the absolute silence, I heard the scraping of a pen writing on the white chalk walls of the cave, held by an invisible hand, and when I came back to my senses, the sound became that of the drill on my molars, and then the stainless steel curette with which they filled the cavities in my teeth with lead.

"Where is your wife?"

I spit and quickly returned back there, to the text that was being drawn out that I deciphered in the glow on the DCA projectors. And what I was reading there- that was the story of my life, as I was ending it in this moment. But when the power of the words began to flicker, I found myself with Hofer leaning above me and saying to me, "There you go you loudmouth. Stopped from betraying us, nein?"

So it was him that had driven me out, pretending that he wanted to take me with him on the Helgoland so that I could no longer be wary of him. He had found out I was spying for the Allies using a classic method: giving false information only to me to see if it would then be transmitted to the enemy. So – except for him – I had been the only one to read Hitler's diary, long excerpts of which the German BBC was now broadcasting to show the Nazi troops how demented their leader had become.

The material Soldaten Calais was using came from a traitor that they were not able to unmask. But as the Führer retreated to the depths of his bunkers in Eastern Prussia, in the wolf's den, or in Bavaria, in Berchtesgaden, the number of suspects diminished. Slowly, the clamp tightened around me.

"It was Lizbeth who recruited you for Admiral Canaris, nein? Then you were sent to that phony mission in Quebec. A friendly gift for Churchill: the head of the killer Himmler had sent him himself. Canaris is dead. Strangled with an E major piano wire. A favor for a music lover."

"You hatched up this scheme with your half-brother Perceval. But he will be punished too. I will see to it myself. I will also make sure you will go down in history as a traitor to your country. The fake invasion plans you gave us cost us thousands of men."

He tore up the films that were dangling on the wire and handed them to the dentist who saluted by clicking his heels.

"Let me introduce you to Doctor Heusenberg," he said, "the Führer's personal dentist. Did you know that after a partial incineration, the jaw is usually the only thing left to identify a corpse? Your mouth will serve the Reich one last time, my dear von Chénier."

Two guards untied me and escorted me to a car that drove a few kilometers in a morning fog that covered us from the bombardiers.

"Follow me," Hofer barked. He slammed the car door and we climbed a monumental staircase, flanked by two somber Breker statues, symbolizing justice and the party, towards the porch with columns defying the bombardments.

The rain, coming from the north, was falling on the blond archangels in black and silver uniforms, legs apart in front of the monumental door, beneath the eagle that held a swastika in its talons. I swallowed the blood that kept pouring out of my gums.

"The rats are fleeing the ship, Hofer said. Kommen Sie, schnell!"

We crossed the grand marble halls of the New Chancellery, finely wrought chandeliers strewn across the ceilings, with complex curves ending in bronze hooks. We exited in a garden. A giant mole had dug a hole. Of the decapitated trees, only stubs of trunks remained.

A hall opened on a rectangular, brownish blockhaus, half-buried underground: the entrance of the bunker. Steel doors. On the first level:

the kitchens, the servants' quarters, Gœbbels' bedroom. Then, at the bottom of the metallic spiral staircase, about ten meters below, a sentinel turned his globular eyes, their cornea a grayish color, on our Ausweiss before opening the airlock to the second bunker, in a pressure of that of ten atmospheres stinking of tobacco and the generator's diesel. The faces seemed to grow tenser and more closed off, as we were getting closer to the Führer.

Electric cables and garden hoses intertwined on the moist ground, in a smell of oil that the loud ventilating system could not get rid of. Soldiers in uniform were crammed in a hallway; they were drunk and stupefied. Hofer gestured for me to enter a small room at the back.

He ordered me to write a detailed confession before my execution. He left me with a ream of paper and a lead pencil.

"And watch it, I want the truth," he said. "None of those extravagant tales you've concocted and then microfilmed for the Propaganda Ministry."

"You will soon meet the one whose fillings you now have. We'll need the dental work of a burnt corpse to identify him. We'll keep you alive until the end."

I write while I wait for them to come get me. A bunk, a netted light bulb and the device I use to microfilm the documents the Führer is still producing, and that they're burning up there in the chancellery's garden as I photograph it. I scribble on the back of the loose sheets they bring me, and I use my free time to insert my story under the Zeiss lens. Discipline is becoming lax: an odor of Schnapps and vomit, cries of voluptuousness and sobs of despair. Götterdämmerung and company.

I talk to myself, I sing in French, no one is paying attention to me, I mobilize the verb's resources, from the abundant saliva to the melody of love, deep baritone voice and then high like a eunuch's, from Wagner to Mozart. God is a heart. When you look at them closely, all human beings are gods: they vibrate with an extraordinary intensity, in their every move, look and breathe. "Alouette, gentille alouette!"

"Alouette, je t'y plumerai!" the voice of my soft, tender, beloved Lizbeth answers from the other side of the wall. The door of my cell opens a little for a moment and then my wife throws herself in my arms. In the torture-induced delirium, did I betray her before that? Her blue dress with white polka dots smells of mould. I want to kiss her, but she hides her face in my shoulder, which she wets, through my shirt, with a warm substance. I think she is crying; I firmly lift her chin: blood is dripping from behind her lips. She smiles bravely, but even before she opens her jaw, I know I will find the traces of Doctor Heusenberg's work. Fortunately, she only had to endure two useless removals of upper-molars. At that moment, she notices that I have also suffered. She takes her hands in mine and makes me sit on the bunk next to her.

"Before I was arrested," she whispers in my ear, "I warned Friedrich. He is already in contact with high elements of the Red Army. They will try everything they can to destroy the tunnel beneath the bunker. They think they will manage it by going through the subway."

"Heraus! Schnell!" A guard enters and pushes us in the hall. It is panic. Odors of vodka and vomit. Sitting in a semi-circle, filthy marshals are listening to a secretary read them their tarot cards. Distraught messengers run, carriers of contradictory orders. In a tiny room, Gœbbels' seven children are freezing on their pillows placed directly on the floor, eyes looking up at their mother, Magda. The six girls' pajamas are pink and the one boy's is blue. When they turn their baby faces toward us, I feel the same pity as I did when a carpenter had cut the flooring in our basement, exposing a litter of young mice still blind, tightly packed and squeaking against one another, searching with their soft and moist noses for their mother's side, who had escaped.

They had only found the cold blade of the shovel that was lifting them and carrying them to the WC's white bowl, towards a long slide to drowning.

Hofer greets Mrs. Gœbbels by leaning his torso and takes her to a corner. From his brief case, he pulls out a beribboned box wrapped in green and red paper: "The promised gift, gnädige Frau," he said. "Candies, for you and your children." She takes off the paper wrapping. I see glass capsules, carefully placed in cotton wool to prevent them from knocking each other.

Lizbeth seems terrorized. Hofer comes back towards us, softly closing the door while saying: "Be good, children." He is exalted: in the last few days, his career got a dizzying ascension. He is now consoling his Minister's children. " Follow me!" he says dryly.

We are now in front of the Führer. Haggard, his eyes bloodshot, rings under them, temples pulsating, purplish tinge, looking like a ghost, on the verge of collapsing his terribly trembling body, he is leaning over a map and is not looking at me. He is wearing a green shirt under a grey pearl tunic, as well as grey pants. A war cross and a gold plate are dangling on his chest. His voice still seems to hold the threads that operate the puppets around him. The badly tightened joint of a garden hose is leaking water on the Turkish rug. Eva Braun comes out of her bath: she wipes the beads of sweat from her forehead with her bathrobe sleeve. Hitler sits on a Louis XV sofa; a strand of hair falls over his forehead.

The woman examines him with the tip of her fingers. And here, did I hurt you? Every spot touched is attached to millions of men dressed in rags, covered in bloody bandages. Long black hair lay next to his navel, that are being lifted by a deaf, blocked breathing relieved by a dry cough, to which echo the thousands of cannons on the surface, that are protecting the sacred breath, this umbilical hole of Berlin, where we are still alive with the rest of the intestinal fauna of the bunker.

The digestion is blocked, those idiots know it, but they will die to protect him. Aida. The hero walled up alive. The woman goes to change in the room next to the boudoir, and comes back wearing a silk strawberry-colored scarf around her neck. She grabs Lizbeth's hands and looks at her in the eyes.

"So, du bist mein Dopplegänger!" she says. Then she shakes her head, turns around swiftly and declares that she will not need this double of herself. She prefers to get it over with right now. Hofer protests to defend his plan, but It is done in vain. He ends up giving in and opening the soundproof double doors to the Führer's private quarters.

Klempka, Hitler's chauffeur, enters. He is carrying a bag of cement and puts it on the floor. Then I am ordered to help him move the furniture that we are pushing, along with the rolled carpet, against the back wall. I am forced to put on the chancellor's clothes: iron cross and a cap with a black visor. A huge concrete block suddenly loosens from the wall, moving with a crash in the desk, scraping the floor, freeing an opening bit by bit through which Hitler disappears, head low, after cold goodbyes to his wife.

She is crying as she comes to sit next to me on the white and blue sofa. She throws her goatskin sandals in front of her and brings her feet under her supple body. She is holding two capsules in the palm of her hand. She brings one to her mouth. I hear the glass crack between her teeth. A violent twitch and she is dead as the bitter hazelnut smell spreads in the stuffy air. Oddly, her body takes the pose of a horse rider, bent in half and her arms stretched in front of her as if her hands held invisible reigns. A muffled discussion continues between Hofer and

Klempka. I think they are trying to determine the angle of the bullet they will shoot in my head, with a Walther 7.65mm, so that it would look like a suicide. Lizbeth silently mouths: "Ich liebe dich!"

When Klempka is about to pull the trigger, we hear a deafening roar and feel the ground tremble beneath our feet. Cries, barks. Hofer catapults himself towards the secret opening. He comes back a few minutes later with the Führer.

"They just blew up the emergency exit," he says to Klempka. "All is lost."

I squeeze Lizbeth's hand and hold back a victorious smile: Friedrich found the tunnel and blew it up just in time. Now Hitler cannot go ahead with his plan. He thinks a victory is still possible. He demands that Steiner's armed group be called; his last hope. After that, he will see. His hunched back and lurching shoulders startle and shake. His head is snuggled between his shoulders like that of a turtle in its shell. The two puppets click their heels. Then he begins to write at the sane time as me, in a notebook identical to the one I took out from under my jacket and in which I am writing this.

I know that soon we will be taken out by the opening through which Hitler came. For now, I continue to observe the pencil that is tracing these lines. Hofer has just left us. He plans on escaping the Surrounded City by barge. He brings the microfilms with him. A massive deception awaits him: every time I recognized Hitler's handwriting, I overexposed the film. Contrary to his hopes, he will have nothing to sell at a high price to future American Nazi relic collectors.

From Lizbeth, I can hear everything, even the story of my death. "You were alive and now you're not. That's how it is," she says with a smile.

But she is talking about something else, about the miracle of space. "Just before, when I was brought here, I felt an enormous, infinite space. There's enough for all of us. It contains all the fragments of nothingness. That's where the B-17s are flying, not here in our heads. Where Christophe is sleeping. Dreaming about us."

I close my eyes and continue to write what Lizbeth is telling me. Everything lights up from the inside, in the soft pulsating of my conscience.

PART TWO

May 7, 1987, Quebec

Dear Christophe,

All my life I have wanted to confess something. But the circumstances – and my cowardice – have prevented me from doing so. I hid the identity of your parents from you, to protect you. What irony! I could not have known you would ruin your life because you believed you were the son of an Anglo-Canadian officer. Or that rebellion against your fake father Perceval would lead you to become a terrorist and rot in a federal prison cell.

I see you again every year, becoming harder, dryer, more unemotional, behind the transparent wall, the grill so low that it forced us to bend forward in a humiliating fashion to talk together, as our hands followed each other on each side of the scratched Plexiglas.

I am your grandmother, but I've loved you as more than a son. Our meetings tortured me: I sometimes wished sickness would prevent me from going to Saint-Vincent-de-Paul on Sundays. I felt guilty of your fate, especially when my psychiatrist explained his theory to me: the nostalgic love for an Acadian mother, dead shortly after you were born, the hate towards a military father, authoritarian and Anglophone seemed to have led you to place a bomb in front of a station, for the sake of the Francophone independence.

If he had known what I did not dare tell you at the time, and later on, when you were freed and you appeared to be so fragile to me: those parents were a fiction maintained by me, would he not have held me responsible for your problems?

As I write these lines now, ten years have gone by since you were let out of prison. I see you are more solid, earning a living as a translator.

But I do not have the courage to tell you the truth face to face. This confession, I agreed to it only because I know you will read it after my death. I will therefore never have to look you in the eye. Even so, I am still hesitating...

Know that your father was von Chénier. Yes, your uncle André. So you are still my grandson. You will also understand the reasons for my discretion. You father being considered a national traitor, I was afraid your life would be ruined. And because I was not taking your parents away from you since they had already disappeared, perhaps dead, in Berlin, in 1945.

When I remarried André-Didier Bouchard in the fall of 1947, I told him everything and asked him to decide what we should do. He begged me not to tell you anything, so as not to harm your psychological state. You know how much the man loved peace. Another engineer, like my poor second husband. And, I might add without any malicious intent, another French Canadian. My father, the colonel, has surely turned in his grave.

But I should not have followed André-Didier's advice: we were building your past on lies, and we could only bring misfortune upon you.

I have many things to tell you about your father: first of all, do not believe what the history books say about him. He was not a traitor to his country, certainly not in Quebec where he fought for the liberation until the very end, with dubious methods and allies, but also with a total and admirable devotion to his cause. But in the end, my son did not betray Canada either, even if he did renounce it as a homeland.

In 1943, and until the end of the war, he had become a double agent for the Allies. His programs seemed odious, calling the French Canadians to lay down their arms, to sign an alliance with Great Germany, and so with the devil, and that everyday on the airwaves of Radio-Berlin served to transmit precious information.

Unfortunately, he made Perceval and I swear absolute discretion, warning us that within the Canadian headquarters there were Nazi traitors who would betray him in Berlin should the slightest rumor about him circulate. And us, he had forced us to compromise ourselves by handing over secret documents. This act that he had demanded in order to save his mission at the Quebec conference, and perhaps as proof of our good faith, would cost Perceval his life. I will tell you how soon.

Towards the end of the war, I do not know exactly when the Germans found out a traitor had infiltrated Gœbbels' entourage and was transmitting spicy and authentic details to the Allies about the Führer's personal life. He became enraged when the BBC mocked his sexual habits. He suspected his closest collaborators and often, the most efficient. He would hit randomly at the smallest doubt. His natural paranoia grew stronger and hindered the conduct of war. Sooner or later, he found your father out, who kept his cool in spite of it all, and continued to encrypt and broadcast his shows.

But on an April day in 1945, Perceval searched the specter of short waves looking for his half-brother in vain. We were mortally worried right away. It was not a power failure or a destruction of the antenna: Radio-Berlin was still broadcasting. But without any explanation, they had replaced the usual Wednesday Quebecer speaker by a German voice. The Nazi propaganda effort in French Canada had abruptly stopped.

Perceval examined the recordings of von Chénier's latest programs without finding anything out of the ordinary. What should he do? Alert his superior? He did not dare. No one at headquarters knew the identity of the propaganda representative for Nazi Germany. Of course your father's name was on a short list of suspects, but they lacked conclusive proof as your uncle and I pretended we did not recognize his voice.

Hence, we were accomplices in more than one way. Of course, after the war, when we would establish who von Chénier was and what great services he had rendered to the homeland, we would be covered in medals. If the Canadian Information Service knew that an unknown informant was using the broadcast towards Canada to communicate with them, they did not know that the mysterious author of these texts encrypted in a childish code would easily break in a few hours, once the Gestapo experts were alerted. They were based on the number of words of the program according to the date. Who was it? The speaker, the director, or the scriptwriter? What character pulled the strings from the shadows?

My worry grew as André's silence prolonged itself. We were watching out for any announcement from the Tass agency about a transfer to the Canadians of one of their own that would have fled through the Nazi lines to take refuge with his wife next to the Soviet heroes. But nothing. On the first of May, at eight in the morning, in the solemn decor of Bruckner's seventh symphony, Radio-Berlin claimed the fake news of the Führer's heroic death in combat with the Bolsheviks. On the seventh of May, the new chancellor, the Great Admiral Dœnitz, signed the surrender of the Reich without any condition.

How could I have known that the first news about André would come from the sea, on board the Helgoland sailboat? Yet, we were alerted when the newspapers reported that the German cutter had beached on reefs in the Chaleur Bay, only to be saved by a Coast Guard duffle-boat up to the harbor in Paspébiac.

The crew had vanished in the woods, and the police was organizing a search across the whole Gaspésie peninsula, because the boat belonged to the Führer. Built in 1936, it had won the Spanish Cup the following year for a rich Hanseatic ship owner, who then had given it to Hitler as a birthday present. He used it for a few short cruises on the North Sea, abundantly filmed by the Propaganda Ministry, and then stationed it in Kiel, next to the U-Boat, under the responsibility of Admiral Dœnitz.

During the war, huge concrete fortifications protected it from the Allies' bombing. And, in May of 1945, the Helgoland escaped ahead of the English troops who could not stop it like they had been ordered to. It headed for the Atlantic, sporting a Swedish flag to pass through the Cuxhaven strait by fooling the enemy's patrol boats. According to the rumors, it was carrying Nazi high dignitaries to South America. It was believed that its low tonnage would allow it to go up the Rio Ocho, to the capital of Paraguay, where General Julius Strœssner would have welcomed representatives of the Third Reich, even if they had fallen from grace.

The American government cabled its ambassador in Asuncion, so that she would exercise a discrete watch over the fluvial port. On the off chance that a few local agents were given the descriptions of Martin Borman and Hitler, whose body was still being searched for in vain. You can hardly imagine the commotion that would be created, in August 1945: the apparition of the Helgoland beached in the Chaleur Bay, fifteen thousand kilometers north of the anticipated location. In the same location, I might add, where your father had landed, two years earlier, for a secret mission in Quebec. But this correlation, only Perceval and I would be able to establish.

Without really believing it much, we were hoping that André had come back to the country with his wife and was preparing to contact us all to organize a meeting with the press and the military organization.

As for the policemen, no matter how much they interrogated the people from the village, no one knew which crew had abandoned "the German's boat" thusly, on its keel, in the middle of the night. A few days after the shipwreck, the body of a German sailor was found at the bottom of a cliff, where a sign now says to the tourists to "let nature follow its course," so that they are not tempted to rescue the agonizing Northern gannets that have foolishly hit their heads on the rocks. The course of nature, the heart of man, the two rarely ever agree, don't you think?

In Kiel, the Helgoland's home base, the British discovered that an important character, carrier of a Führerbefehl (order written by Hitler's very hand), had gone to sea with two crewmembers a few days before the German surrender, accessing that the name of the ship did not appear in the departure registry.

And then there was that phone call. It is possible you might remember that cool evening at the end of August: you were already seven years old. A swarm of wasps had attacked you. I was tending to your stings with a pink ointment that you hated the smell of. Your face swollen, you could barely see or speak. We were talking with Perceval on the porch of the country house that I had inherited from your father's father (my successive widowhoods require this precision).

I was holding you on my lap: a woolen blanket shielded us from the cold air that was coming from the nearby river. Beneath the rumble of the rapids, we could hear the blocks of the drive crash against each other in a dry and chaotic rhythm like the gunshots at the end of a fight.

I showed you the bare light bulb that dangled among the spirals of flypaper. "It's your grandfather's dam that is lighting us," I explained. "But the *bastards* of high finances stole it from us."

"You'll make a revolutionary out of that child!" Perceval said. He did not know that I was already signed up in the Communist Party and that I was acting deliberately. You had fallen asleep in my arms. Your uncle quietly put down the pieces on the chessboard in the position taken on the fortieth move of a match he was playing against your father for nearly two years.

When Perceval had "discovered" a code in von Chénier's speeches and had signaled it to his superiors, he had hidden the existence of another number that announced a gambit of the queen from them. He encrypted his reply, a Sicilian Defense, in the Radio-Canada bulletin that he wrote and that the Canadians were using to communicate with their enigmatic informant.

Out of superstition, we left the chair empty in front of the black pieces. We would turn on the shortwave radio; the speaker of which covered in green fabric and mahogany marquetry, seemed to be from beyond the grave and not from across the Atlantic. From there, André's voice came to us, insolent and declamatory; so familiar despite the magnetic distortions. His faraway computing came to move the wooden pieces on the folding table that was still sticky in some places from the strawberry jam you had dropped on it.

But on that August evening of 1945, Radio-Berlin was not broadcasting anymore. On the usual frequency, we could only hear the crackling of emptiness. The position of the match had not changed in three months.

At twenty-seven, Perceval was dying from blood cancer, which he kept from me, but that I knew about thanks to his doctor's confiding in me. In the middle of his emaciated face, already shadowed from inside as if by death, his cobalt blue eyes, slit like almonds, moved with a vigor as intense as his calculations on the white and black squares.

"I lost!" he said, standing up after a while. "André can checkmate me in three moves. Unstoppable!"

"Maybe he didn't see it…"

"I did!"

A great sadness then washed over me. The true loser was me, who could feel two sons slipping away from life with a force as irresistible as the one that had brought them to this world through my spread legs.

It was then that the telephone sounded two brief rings and then the long one that was reserved for us on the line we shared with our neighbors. "Sure… Sure… Right away!" Perceval said in a blank voice before hanging up. It was Captain Dansereau, of the provincial police. He wanted to see him immediately about your father.

"That boat, the Helgoland, brought us some news," he settled to say.

The gold crest with Her Majesty's coats-of-arm shone on his khaki cap that he adjusted by pulling on the visor. He slipped his whip under his left elbow and crouched to hug you. The copper buttons made you give out a cry.

"You're hurting me, daddy!"

Then, he pushed my chin up with his outstretched index finger and smiled at me saying, "See you, kiddo!"

Turning his back to us, he left, went down the three rotten steps of the porch, crossed the wet lawn while whistling "Slow boat to China," then turned right towards his Jeep and disappeared behind the beveled glass encased in the front door that had remained ajar and that a resin-scented wind made oscillate on its hinges. The lights went on and momentarily banished our reflections from the window: a forty-four-year-old woman with red hair and who was too thin was holding a black haired boy against her hip; his face swollen by wasp stingers.

Like in the story of the Holy Grail, Perceval had left his mother to become a knight, or rather to remain one. But at the end of his run, redemption was not waiting for him, only Captain Dansereau who had told him he had received "guests from Germany" and refused to go into more detail over the phone.

I only fell asleep in the morning, with Veronal and scotch. It took some time for your cries to pierce through my anesthesia and make way into my nightmares. I put on my bathrobe and ran to the shores of the Jacques-Cartier River.

A stranger was sitting at the end of the floating quay, legs dangling, shoulders strong, but lurching from fatigue. He was making ripples that made you laugh with a cable attached to the back barge where you were jumping for joy in the middle of the rapids. Only the cable, which he held nonchalantly, was preventing you from following the current and killing yourself on the rocks that were invisible from here at the bottom of that line, where the river comes to an abrupt stop after having passed the dam's dyke.

I screamed. He stood up with difficulty and turned around to face me: in his fifties, a wrinkled blue suit with white chevrons, a red tie with white polka dots, browns eyes that did not blink and that were sizing me up without haste from beneath a felt hat that hid them. His massive jaw was biting down on a curved pipe with a Bavarian styled earthen bowl. He pointed it out to me and said, "Nice work, right? A friend from Berlin gave it to me…"

Contrary to my expectation, he was not speaking German, but French with the accent from the Saint-Roch district in Quebec. He was smoking tobacco that had an acrid smell that remains, to me, the smell of death. I was very afraid for you, of course, because he had just to open his hands with the rope, which he hid behind for you to go and hurt yourself on the rocks in front of your grandfather's old office; but I also feared for Perceval from whom I still had no news.

I could feel, the void between the slick and humid planks of the quay under my bare feet. In a hysterical voice, I ordered you to sit. You grumbled but obeyed, and then you started playing with an empty can in the water at the bottom of the hull.

"That child is soaked. You have to bring him back to me," I told the visitor.

"You think so? To raise real men, women are worth nothing... But you don't have to be afraid of me; I am Captain Dansereau of the provincial police. Sit down, I have some really bad news."

"You dirty Nazi bastard!"

He closed his eyes for a moment, furrowing his brow like someone suffering from a migraine.

"So you already know... It was a good thing I came for a visit. My German friend was right. He's a perceptive man. Compliant, but it's best not to make him brood. Your sons abused his patience. They played a nasty trick on him. So he insisted on expressing his annoyance. First in Berlin... I don't think you'll be hosting von Chénier and his wife. And then here, last night, with Perceval... The poor man had an accident. He was driving too fast. He missed a turn near the Éboulements. From the top of a cliff: it is unforgiving. Despite the prevention campaigns we keep multiplying, drivers continue to lack caution. It makes for widows and orphans like you and your grandson... Actually, when I told him about your isolated house in front of the rapids, my friend got worried about the risks of drowning. But I said I would come to give you cautionary advice. And what do I see when I get here? Young Christophe venturing out on the waters, who I've just saved, while his grandmother is sleeping off the scotch... Don't protest. I went up to your room and I smelled your breath just before..."

Despite the summer sun, I was shivering more and more as that man spoke; my teeth were clattering and my legs were quivering so much that I had to kneel down. Looking satisfied, he tied the cable to a moss-covered pole, emptied his cold pipe in the river and said, after a sigh, "There. I'm leaving you. With the last recommendation of a man of the law: don't abuse alcohol. It loosens the tongue and impudent ramblings make my friend brood."

His steel heels sounded hollow as he made his way back to solid grounds; he passed me on my left, caressed the back of my neck and said I looked "charming like this," walked away and then came back towards me and gave me an envelope. Since I stayed with my arms dangling, my gaze vacant, he threw it in front of me:

"The Germans wanted me to give you that."

Later, when I had heard his car drive away at the end of the wood path, and after I had brought you back to the house, shivering and suddenly scared, I read the document left by Dansereau. It was written in a gothic character and described three moves by the black chess ponds that, in the match between my two sons, led to a checkmate against Perceval.

I did not have a choice. I had to keep quiet. I could not expose Dansereau, a policeman beyond suspicion and friend of power, without exposing my own role and accusing myself. At the time, high treason still led directly to the gallows. So I acted surprised – my despair, on the other hand, was entirely real – first when I was told about Perceval's death, and then when the newspapers published the true identity of von Chénier: this André Chénier, whose family was obviously interrogated.

I was not ready to risk my life, and yours even less, to prove to a scandalized public, thirsty for vengeance, that my son was in reality a hero. It was soon forgotten that there had been an ally informant working for the Canadian programming of Radio-Berlin. I was happy that the scandal hadn't stained Perceval, and that I could talk about your "father" whose name of Perkins you would take to protect your true origin.

Since I was keeping quiet, Dansereau did not worry me any longer. Neither did his threats nor his caresses. Toward the end of the 1960s, when you were starting to serve your sentence, I learned he had died in a particularly horrible manner, which appeared like the only real existing proof of God that I know: he fell into a tank of sulfuric acid during a fight with strikers in a factory of paint products.

You will find it interesting to know what happened to the Helgoland, the boat on which the "German friend" had come to us. Endless judicial discussions established that since they could not give the sailboat back to its original owner, Canada had to consider it as 'spoils of war.' So the navy inherited it, re-baptized it Pickle, and transformed it into a boat school for its cadet officers. It is now rotting in the port of Halifax and there is talk of selling it in an upcoming auction.

Who was Dansereau's German friend? I do not know. Forty years later, as I am writing down these lines, all these people are probably dead and buried.

Together with this letter, you will receive my written will, dated and signed. You will see that I am not leaving much and that I spent almost everything my third husband had left me in the West Indies. Will you hold that against me too?

Your grandmother who adores you,

Virginia Perkins
34 Saint-Sacrement Street
Quebec

PART THREE

NOTEBOOK ONE

At the age of forty-five, Christophe Perkins received a letter from his grandmother that was like a smack behind the head didn't wake him as much as it shook him up. And so were explained the mysteries of his childhood: the notes his "father" would scribble down quickly while listening to the radio; the never-ending game of chess he was pretending to play against himself; Virginia's anger when, later in his teenage years, he dared to condemn his Nazi "uncle" von Chénier. "Shut up," she had yelled. "You don't know who you're talking about!"

They kept lying to me, Christophe thought on that September morning, as he sat in the front of an outboard motorboat, at the port in Halifax, a month after Virginia's death. He saw the wheat silos and the oil tanks scroll by in front of the grey city that layered up tone on tone through the fog. Getting farther from the Transportation Ministry's quay, the office worker – his face dull beneath the bright yellow of his fisherman's raincoat – sped up, covering the sound of the ringing bells of the buoys with his engine's backfire.

"There she is!" The office worker yelled as he pointed to the front. Christophe turned around and in order not to lose his balance, leaned on the bow of the boat that was jumping on the waves. In the brisk wind, his angular face – usually pale – was reddening, accentuating the lightness of his blond, tussled hair. His teary eyes were studying the Helgoland like one watches a prey. The black mast and the sharp keel formed a cross with their reflection on the oily sea.

The engine stopped. With a muffled thud; the canoe hit the pleasure craft that was heeling portside quite a bit.

"You're taller than I am," said the office worker. "You go first."

Christophe pulled himself up on the bridge and tied the rope he'd caught to a cleat. With the glow of a flashlight, they visited the flooded hold of Hitler's old yacht; the water, which was seeping through the poorly caulked planking, was up to their thigh boots. But they did not find any major water entry. The unusual fairing material – tempered steel – alone revealed the ship had long ago belonged to the Kriegsmarine before carrying Dansereau's German friend to Canada.

Had the killer left any trace of his passing?

The engine, though, dated back no more than ten years, as with the autopilot, the radar and the UHF device. The Helgoland, Christophe thought, would only be seaworthy after long and costly repairs, but hitting the shell with his screwdriver proved that beneath the thick layer of algae and seashells, the timber was still good.

"I'm buying it!" he told the office worker.

Back in the office of the port's management, he closed the transaction by paying the twelve thousand dollars the Canadian Marine was asking for. "Half of the pitiful fortune Virginia left me." Then he returned to his hotel, the Duke of York, which cigars used to stink out ages ago.

"I'll shoot myself in the head." This sentence was constantly coming back to him, and every time, he could almost feel the cold cannon of his Colt 38 that he had left in Montreal, in the right drawer of his desk, where he could grab it as easily as one grabs a dictionary, lift his eyes over the bricks darkened by pollution of the walls of Saint-Joseph boulevard, towards the grey matter of any cloud. In a tired gesture, like with a fly, he chased away the idea of suicide. It seemed it haunted him more frequently since Virginia's death.

Not only had he not inherited the magnificent house on Saint-Sacrement street, too heavily mortgaged, that he wanted, nor the capital that would have allowed him to burn the thousands of pages of federal rules that he had to translate from English to French in order to survive every year, but the will of his priceless grandmother – may she burn in hell – was able to dispossess him of what little he had left: his past. The dead ceased the open wound and she transformed childhood memories in as many fake bills. Fake, this authoritarian father, that demanded that the corners of his bedspread fall at a right angle on the linoleum of his childhood bedroom, that insisted on talking in a terribly shaky and anglicized French under the false pretense that his mother – the equally false Acadian – wanted it this way.

All at once it seemed his rebellion against the British institutions, personified by this Perceval Perkins, against the passport that asked, still today, in the name of "the Queen, for the interested authorities to please grant him the right of way," was losing all its political sense.

Should he rebuild his past like you regain capital? He did not have a choice. The price to pay for those who refuse to give a burial to their own was too heavy. The dead, who constitute the essence of thought, do not talk. His life was falling away though the void of his origins like when one pulls on a plug in a bathtub. He did not have too much of the Cutty Sark scotch he was drinking directly from the bottle to keep a little bit of liquid in his veins. The phone rang on the bedside table, next to the bed that was drifting off under the ceiling reddened by the rhythm of the neon signs.

"This is Anthony O'Reilly. I was given the name of your hotel at the port management office. I'm at the bar."

The man was wearing a Basque beret over white, thick, curly hair that only made his physiognomy look even more stubborn where an elusive irony floated. He was drinking a beer. In front of the free sofa at his table, a glass of scotch was waiting for Christophe.

"It's Cutty Sark. The barman said it's the only thing you drink. Cheers! OK… Listen, I came here with a good business proposition for you. I'm operating a dockyard in Paspébiac. Because of this stupid fog, my flight was delayed and I missed the auction for the Helgoland this morning. I'm offering you five thousand dollars more than you paid."

"No," Christophe quickly replied. "The boat isn't for sale. For personal reasons make it that it is priceless to me."

The Irishman gave him an inquiring look that remained unanswered. "You saw the state of the hull?"

"I know. I'll take care of it myself."

"Well then let me offer my dock for the repairs. I'll take care of the towing as well. We'll have to install a pump in the hold or it'll sink."

"And what is this generous offer for?"

"I'm the owner of a hotel in Paspébiac. It's far from the tourist circuit. I thought of making an original attraction out of the Helgoland. Visiting Hitler's old boat- that could interest people... So, when you don't need it, maybe I could rent it from you monthly..."

"Why not?"

The two men agreed on a price. O'Reilly called his coaster to tow the Helgoland up to the dockyard in Paspébiac where it was brought to the dry dock. There, the hold finally dried out, Christophe searched in vain for a clue on the identity of Dansereau's German friend. Also, using tar, he began to caulk the oak boards that had been cut from the Black Forest in 1936, carefully squared off by the Bremen cabinetmaker, coated in varnish, twined like the threads of an enormous wire that attached the past to the Helgoland. The boat slept and remembered.

When replacing the oak marquetry, he discovered behind a rotten panel, under the sink drain, a metallic cylinder embossed with a Prussian eagle. At first he thought it was a pornographic film that the crew of the little sailboat would watch when the boat belonged to the Royal Canadian Navy.

Sucking on the finger he had cut on the side of the cap, he unrolled the bobbin in front of a lamp, his eyes blinking before the minuscule rectangles: microfilmed text too small to be deciphered with the naked eye! To do so, he would have to use one of the viewers at the National Library when he would return to Montreal. So then the German, despite his caution, had left evidence behind. Surely he thought that the Helgoland, torn by the reefs, would sink with bodies and goods.

Soon, Christophe was able to put the boat back on the waves, and he invited O'Reilly onboard, who had helped him replace beams and weld rivets, and whose hotel he had been staying at.

They sat on the seat in the cabin that still smelled of varnish. Behind the portholes, a meter above, the edge of the quay was rounding up in the fog underlining the cannery like a bold trait. Christophe felt homesick for Germany, homesick for his mother, present in his thoughts like a German suffix.

After his fifth glass, he who would never confide in anyone began to talk about how he had committed an act of terrorism twenty years ago.

"Here's to the IRA!" cheered his partner, as he drank his glass in one fell swoop.

In his college laboratory, Christophe had stolen three flasks, wrapped them up in a newspaper and placed them in his briefcase. The smell of rotten eggs. The perfectly circular hole carved by the nitric acid he had thrown in his bedroom wall. His burnt right palm, the yellowish and dried skin that peeled in layers from having grabbed a bottle with a light sulfur mist on it. The tar-like mix; inert like ink. Then the surprise of ebullition, the expectorant chemical groan in the July air, a red mushroom the size of the house. But he had forgotten to add a coil to disperse the vapors.

He fixed his mistake. He built a tube of nitro; it looked like a genie in a bottle, which he placed on the rails of the commuter train. The vibrations set off the explosion well before the arrival of the locomotive. No deaths, a few light injuries, but mostly a whole lot of fear. His war had begun.

From extreme right to extreme left: the classic family portrait, just as the psychiatrist had abundantly explained about his uncle.. He was able to survive because he was one hundred and eighty-five centimeters tall, and he was working as an assistant librarian. He made walls with books and weights.

"I didn't have a choice in there. I had to bring it all back to the question of strength."

"I know exactly what you're talking about," O'Reilly said. "I did some time in Belfast too. For the same reasons."

They listened to the sails flap, they breathed in the smell of rotten wood from the quay. There were shards of the moon on the waves and the world stopped in the middle of the bay. Christophe wiped off the excess saliva from his lips.

"And now you live like a dead man," the Irish said. "I find that very sad… Forgive me for talking to you like that. But I can see that this whole story is killing you. It's a poison for you, isn't it? Your parents must've really loved each other. They should have separated because of the war. But your father preferred to betray his country. And you in all this? They left you behind."

"They didn't have a choice!"

"You really think that? My parents would have dragged us to hell rather than be separated from us."

"In any case, my father wasn't a traitor. In any other country, he would even have been a hero. In Quebec he had to be a double agent, and he became one."

"You know what you have to do? You have to avenge your parents."

"My parents abandoned me when I was two years old; I don't owe them anything. I don't owe anything to my country either. I did twenty years in jail for it and when I got out, I saw that it didn't even exist!"

"You're all fucked up, man," the Irish said as he gave him a solid slap on the shoulder. The day after the defeat of the referendum on the independence project, Christophe indeed thought he had lived in and defended a land of legend. He did not have any truths to defend, only fiction before the universal void.

He earned a living as a translator. He had abandoned all his friends. They no doubt had reason to sing in a total absence of political ideas. He wanted to be able to forget his soul, his pride, his ambition; to hurt himself in poverty, the inner desert. He wanted to take his car and run up his credit card. In California. So he did.

It was in that moment that an official voice had chosen to dryly announce that his grandmother had passed away. A heart attack at the age of eighty-five: a name deleted from the social security computer, a room freeing up in an old folks' home, the family to notify so they could retrieve the deceased's personal effects and organize the funeral.

No tears on this statistical incident. But the death of his grandmother Virginia had cut the last link he had to this grey, sour city. A squirrel was running on a wire over the neighboring school, its days marking a beat with the bell: subway, tunnels, hot wind, a hideous tower with a blue sign with a white fleur-de-lis. Her personal belongings: a trunk in the basement garage. Her letter: your parents are not your parents. Her will: she made him his universal legatee and asked to be incinerated and buried with her two sons. To fulfill her wishes, he would have to search for a father who had disappeared in Germany forty-five years ago.

Wilted, wrinkled, shriveled up in a purple dress with a lace collar. Her death allowed him to love the one who had raised him once again. He made the arrangements with the funeral hall. The metallic urn he was given looked like a bombshell. It had to be changed. He transferred the ashes into an anonymous plastic thermos and stuck her photo on the red plastic cap. He could not decide where to bury her, so he kept her in a cabinet.

He had to sell the Victorian house on Saint-Sacrement Street. He lived there a few weeks: the time to find a buyer. He found the only photo of his real parents. Taken on the porch of the Anglican church of Quebec, on Perceval and Marie's wedding day, Marie, the Acadian from Halifax. The newlyweds triumphed in the foreground, eyes mere slits from the sun's violent light. He, strapped in his uniform and his national motto "God is my right," and she, dreaming and frail, her waist girded by the dress with a train.

Behind, a few steps higher, in the shadow of the bell tower: the couple that had created him. Relentlessly, he searched their faces to read the signs of their future fate. His father, a twenty-something redhead, whose portrait he had seen in history books: withdrawn lower jaw, thick lips and a slender neck that betrayed a weakness and sentimentality he was trying to hide with a stubborn pout and his arms crossed over a black velvet suit with thick white stripes. The lesser son, Christophe thought before the adoration Virginia expressed as she looked at Perceval.

The image of his mother, whom he was seeing for the first time, caused him genuine shock. He did not understand what neither Virginia's letter nor the reading of the few snippets about his father had explained: why had von Chénier, leaving his son and country, thrown himself towards the dangerous perils of a hysterical Germany? A simple glance at Lizbeth was enough for him. In this amateur shot, she emanated as much beauty as the mysterious silent movie stars. Great eyes partially hidden by the fringe of her hair. His mother. She held on to her lover's arm with such fondness, but the look she was giving Virginia was not tender.

The Irish whistled between his teeth as he gave him the photo back. "What a babe. But your Virginia, at eighty, she wasn't imagining things a little?"

"You want to see what I found here?" Christophe asked. He got up and felt around the cache under the sink, pulling out the cylinder with the Prussian eagle that he placed between them on the cabin table.
"What is it?" O'Reilly asked.

"Nazi microfilms," he answered, feeling slightly nauseous. Then he climbed up the ladder that led to the cockpit, staggered across the deck and then without thinking, threw himself in the sea. He emptied his lungs and sank, oh, the wonderful hushed fall through the freezing water that dragged him to the limit of his burning lungs, that suddenly blew up like the bolt of an air rifle, and reluctantly brought him back to the surface, eyes and mouth full of salt. Leaning over him, the Irish was smiling.

"You see that you don't have a choice. You have to settle this. Or kill yourself. See you!"

He put the bottle of Smirnoff at his feet and climbed the ladder up to the quay. Christophe changed and lay on the deck. The trawlers' superstructures shone over the dark mass of hulls. To the left, a sandy beach stretched between the bay and the Barachois; on the horizon, the low coast of New Brunswick. He pulled up the collar of his loden and traced the railing that surrounded the ship with his thumb where the plate glass had made a swastika appear, engraved in the oak.

He fell unconscious and woke up on his bunk around eleven in the morning, terribly hungry and thirsty. The Irish had to bring him back in the cabin in the early morning. Christophe turned on the radio: the navy fleet had just sailed off to board and inspect refugee boats off the coast of Newfoundland. Canada is a clean country and intends on remaining as such.

He did not have the courage to heat up a can of food in the kitchen that lightly lulled. He listened to the water splashing, the flat sound of the hull when it softly hits the tires attached as buffers to the quay that he climbed on the worm-eaten ladder. He packed his bags, wrapping the cylinder containing the microfilms in his clothes, then, in the sun, he left behind him the smooth, slender silhouette of the Helgoland. He went up the deserted road. A salty scent rose up from a marsh surrounded by wild grass, in the middle of which stood a broadcasting antenna, held in place by steel cables and attached to the ground by a log pontoon.

Quickening his pace, he crossed the bridge over the Barachois and climbed the slope towards the steep forest between the bay and the national road that followed from the top of the cliffs; the coast's rugged edges. At the end of a path of water-filled ruts where the dead trembled over the glow of the sun, he found the Irish's hotel with its three floors of openwork design turrets and its caryatid moldings.

"The boss isn't around?" he asked the waitress after having ordered a kyr.

"Here I am!" the Irish answered. A pair of binoculars dangled from his neck. He had seen a whale with its three babies: blue with fins marbled in black, and he thought he could still hear the echo of songs produced by the biggest mouth on the planet, that whistling the other titans were picking up on thousands of kilometers away. It reminded him of the sound of a sonar on the hull of a submarine.

"I would've liked to be a whale," he said. "Diving at the bottom of the seas, only to surface one ocean later."

Christophe handed him a set of keys. "I'm leaving the boat in your care. I have accounts to settle."

"With the living or the dead?"
"I don't know. If I'm not back in six months, the Helgoland is yours. Can you drive me to the station in three hours?"

In the car, the Irishman, visibly eager to be on more secrets, did not stop watching him from the corner of his eye, but Christophe remained silent. He was being smothered beneath three centuries of treason, defeats and surrenders; his history was written in invisible ink, or in smoke signals. What does an aborted nation dream of? Their agony is discreet, civil, Americanized, but they continue to die through video clips, comic books and free trade. He would have liked to sit with von Chénier and talk to him. But he was dead, murdered, with no one to avenge him. And his absence tormented Christophe as much as his imaginary ridiculed and renounced country. He could not build anything on emptiness; he fell into it, that is all. All that remained was for him to live in that fall, slow and beautiful; to slow it down.

Perhaps, Christophe thought that the Irish could understand him since he did not belong to the triumphant people, with high and clear verbs, that act out their plays on the stakes of history, that move forward with their hands on their hips, with their tutelary god, immense and flamboyant in the night above them; people he admired, as his own were floating in marshy indecision, leaving him an orphan of time, like an unborn fetus; not giving him any leverage to lift the crushing, enigmatic world.

"The best," the Irish said as though he were reading his thoughts, "would be to never be born. Believing you exist is the first mistake. Where are you going like that?"

"Montreal. I have a translation job to do."

"On the microfilms?"

O'Reilly braked and parked on the shoulder of the road. He got out and walked to the trunk, which he opened, and then he waited for Christophe to join him.

"Look in your suitcase," he said.

Before he even unscrewed the cylinder to notice that the microfilms inside were blank, Christophe had figured out the trick the other must have played on him, probably while he lay drunk dead on the deck.

"Where are they?"

"In Halifax. I lied to you. I wasn't trying to buy the boat, not for me, but for a client: a German who didn't have the time to come to Canada. He called me at the dock. I took his offer. He transferred the necessary funds into my account. With a generous commission. He told me he was collecting the items that had belonged to Hitler."

With his back to him, O'Reilly had sat on a rock in front of a bushy, steep slope that went all the way down to the Chaleurs Bay. He was throwing gravel on the corrugated tin of an open sewer.

"He called me last week. I didn't like his tone when he said: 'So you have failed in purchasing the Helgoland?' He explained that it wasn't the boat that interested him so much as a metallic cylinder hidden under the sink. And if something were to happen to you, it wouldn't bother him. I would even get an additional reward, a bonus like in those times in Ireland. The bastard knew of my terrorist past… I told him: 'Hell no! That guy is my friend.' But I didn't want any trouble with that German. So I mailed him the microfilms."

"And why are you telling me all of this?"

"You would've found out when you went to Montreal. You would've known it was me and I don't want any trouble with you either. And ever since you told me your story, I understood that the bastard was the same as the one from forty-five. The trouble with modern medicine: these Nazis are able to live incredibly long… So I have a present for you: the address where I shipped the microfilms in Berlin. Likely to a fake company name… Eckel und Schmidt, Import-Export. Here."

O'Reilly gave him a matchbook on which he had scribbled the information and closed the trunk of the old Ford.

"I don't know what the guy's name is. But I'd advise you to take care of him before he takes care of you. He probably knows a lot of people who would do what I refused to. Especially since he thinks you had the time to read the contents of the microfilms."

They shook hands on the platform of the station. The train rolled along the back country, punctuated by french-fry stands, topless bars, rivers as brown and as foamy as a Guinness, high voltage cancerous iron pylons, giant yellow 'M's under which the McDonald's clowns distributed the minced meat wafers to their kneeling followers, mini-golf courses surrounded by barbed wire and decorated with multicolored plastic flags, DC-3, Boeing; Constellations with their wings cut off and turned into discos, bushes wrapped in Glad bags. The usual magic sowed in a mess across the continent.

In Montreal, Christophe began to study German intensively. He had a knack for languages and he knew that in three weeks he would have the necessary basic vocabulary for a trip. These foreign sounds, through which an element of meaning passed, drawing another universe bit by bit, where night and fog took a sinister form when called Nacht und Nebel; where barbwire attached to pylons that curved toward a vast field of fine gravel could be defined, harnessed detainees dressed in striped jumpsuits and caps that were pulling road rollers that crushed the rocks and made walking easy on the boots, as they went up the center lane, from the administrative center, and they walked between the shacks, eyes riveted on the pines that moved lightly, at the back of the camp to the left fore of the crematory.

Could we free ourselves from the errors of history? Was the dream of national liberation – his and his father's – not already skewed to begin with? In April 1933, the most brilliant partisans of independence had given troubling speeches, in the Gesù hall. The Hitlerian persecutions against the Jews? Imagine! His grandfather, the electrical engineer, was in the room with his two sons and he was applauding the speaker: "The bitch's tail in Germany cannot be stepped on without its bark being heard in Canada."

He had never really known his father. Of all the historical figures from Quebec, he was the one that had been pushed back into the shadows. Von Chénier only appeared in small characters in the footnotes of History books, perhaps because he personified the tendency of these people to betray themselves more than anyone else.

The central government had forcibly mobilized French Canada, which had massively protested the participation in the war during the referendum of 1940. The Prime Minister of Quebec, Duplessis, lost his right to oppose the war. He had been forbidden access to the radio in the middle of the electoral campaign. His opponent won. During the armistice, Camillien Houde, the mayor of Montreal, was freed from the concentration camp, where he had been withering away for four years for having publicly opposed the conscription. Medals were distributed to the heroes, pensions to the widows and von Chénier was consigned to oblivion. The victory that won over absolute evil would forgive the slight injustice that had been committed against its people.

His mother had an arrest warrant floating over her for being a native of an enemy country since 1939. But they could close the case no more on her than they could on his father. They had both disappeared and the official investigation stopped there. As for him, he decided it would start that day.

Without hesitating, and despite the fact that the purchase of the Helgoland had seriously eaten at his inheritance, he decided to leave for Germany. Nothing in his own country mattered to him anymore. You cannot command feelings. He was afraid of dying from a defeatist overdose. He had been taught fear and he did not know how to get rid of it.

NOTEBOOK TWO

At Mirabel, a haughty, imperious voice interrupted the background piano: "Second call for the Lufthansa flight to Berlin." This was a mass-produced airport female speaker: mass-produced in Taiwan. Nickel pipes formed cubes and pyramids over the bar where the beer went stale. About fifty country flags hung from the ceiling, forever immobile in the still air.

"We ask you to please buckle your seatbelts…" Elbow jabs from the neighbors. Honks, roars, take off! The passengers were sweating, while faking calm like the sensation of an elevator going up when the guts contract into nothingness. It was turning into a projectile that could not touch anything from the world below, neither women nor child, without tearing them to shreds.

Wearing a green Tyrolean hat, his neighbor to his left, a motivational psychologist from Ottawa, had been living in anxiety since his twin brother's death. He was raising his children in English to take revenge on his separatist mother who had thrown a knife at his head. "That, that's Germany," an old man from Munich said pointing to a piece of rye bread on his plastic plate. Teutonic Eucharist. A Vietnamese man was pulling his hair out, fistfuls at a time; the flight attendant gave him a sedative. "It happens every time; a lot of people can't stand the lack of space in coach."

Christophe pushed the lock and the ceiling light of the WC lit up. His eyes red, he smiled to himself in the soap and cologne-stained mirror. Solitary connivance that was re-establishing his lost fragmented identity. Everything was changing, except for that wild and weary look in the mirror. Narcissist bewitchment.

Blue sanitizer spun at the bottom of the toilet bowl. Another sleepless night. There was not a clean spot left on the towel. He had to wipe himself with the others' filth. When he came out of the cabin, a female passenger smiled at him. Green eyes, high cheekbones. She offered him a cigarette. "I'm an antiquary," he said. "I specialize in Prussian earthenware. Very rare after all these wars. You?" Dancer. She was on tour in Germany.

A brief sleep restored his balance with the outside and lightened his dreams. The lights were turned off and the attendant unrolled the small screen. Burnt rubber and hardened arteries had the same smell in his mind like a tribute to pay to hasten towards cardiac arrest. He changed seats to contemplate the coast of Ireland, bleeding beneath the sun's stabs. London passed under the right wing. Europe was rushing. Is there a single safe place, safe from the past? He was chasing it, like a burlesque mustached dictator in a video labyrinth.

Christophe was thinking about what the Irish had told him, to come up with a plan, to go from one small gear to the next. The stratosphere was yelling like a perforated lung over the apoplectic Alps.

The wind was shaking the plane; his neighbor was rubbing his groin with a careless index and raised his elbow to drink the last bit of cola: an ice cube was hiding a part of Mont Blanc. "Ladies and gentlemen, kindly refrain from smoking." The landscape was coming up on them like a big hand coming down on the plane. The hangers on the side of the runway scrolled by at high speed. The red firemen, the yellow hills, the grey fuel tanks.

This was a science-fiction-like airport created by a Prussian architect. In the insomniac morning of jetlag, he saw his mother's ancestral homeland. Berlin awaited him! He yawned behind the wheel of his rental Opel. Fifteen minutes and he would arrive at the Müller pension-house hotel. He hung his suits in the closet to smooth them out. A one-hour nap and this breaded and fried thing called a 'Kotelette.'

It is here, on the steps of the Empire that the NATO steps stopped. Checkpoint Charlie. The Brandenburg Gate that perfectly encased the golden angel on the tower of victory in its arches. To the right, the Reichtag, a Soviet barrack, a mobile canteen, recently planted little trees, ditches full of scrap metal, mobile homes, blue ribbons, red poles. In the parking lot, two hares were running beneath the cars. On the radio, Aida sang that she only loved her hero in the grave and that she wanted to warm him up in the entrails of the earth. Reuter Platz. The 17 Juli Strasse was lost in the horizon, larger than the Champs-Élysées.

Instead of the glass towers, he imagined his father's Berlin of forty years earlier: gutted out kitchens where they ate in the rubble, the survivors addresses written in chalk on the walls, skating at the winter palace, the water collected from the fountain with a bucket, the cows in the streets, the requisitioned bicycles, the skeletons in the subway, the canal that was crossed on a raft, the straw sandals, the labors of the Wilhelm II Cathedral in the middle of Berlin, the ripped out pipes that hung from the walls.

To get to the address O'Reilly had given to him, he crossed the Tiergarten by foot, under the dark bolts of the naked trees against the cold October sky. Since his departure from Montreal two days earlier, he had only slept a few hours- a light and feverish sleep. He had ripped so much skin off from around his nails that a lot of his fingers were bleeding. His ulcer was burning, despite the gulps of hydroxide he drank directly from the bottle that he was holding like a weapon inside his trench coat pocket. To chase the pain away, he exercised breathing slowly through his lips, which were sucking in the air that smelled of mud.

Against the reddish and sandy soil, he imagined Lizbeth under the flash of the phosphorus bulbs or bombs, photographed underneath the same oaks while she attempted to flee with von Chénier. This Berlin that would become their grave.

Suddenly, at the end of the asphalt path, between two bushes, a grey form roared toward him, before bouncing off the grilled fence separating them. The furious barking of the wolf dog echoed until the dry order that was barked by a Soviet guard who had been leaning on the fence for a minute to look at him with his expressionless eyes under his fur hat. Then he turned back and resumed his goose-like mechanical walk, in front of a gigantic image of himself: the thirty meter-high statue the Russians had erected to the glory of their soldiers, right in front of the Brandenburg Gate, and where the Siberians kept the sacred flames and the young Asians swept the ground.

He should have died then, he thought, at the end of a long walk on Unter den Linden Avenue, heading for Moscow, stepping past the squabble, not stopping at the soldiers' warnings, to a final fall, face against the sidewalk: his inner night turning white.

He had made a mistake. The address of Eckel und Schmidt VG was really on the left at the end of this road, but to the East. Back to the

Opel. Two hours later, stopping at Checkpoint Charlie, in front of the reptilian mask of a Feldgrau border agent who was moving a mirror mounted on a buggy under the car, making sure the books on the seat were for Christophe's personal use only, that the onboard radio was only for receiving and not emitting and that he was receiving the twenty-five marks for the twenty-four-hour visa the RDA granted.

It came from the vital body, without eyes or ears, only muscular and nervous, with the rhythm of blood to the mouth. There was no means to stop, to stand still. The Shapeless was changing every other second, taking a name and a hat to salute him with a kepi and signaling him to move forward. To the East like to the West, the puppets did not stop parading to give him emotions.

He was pulling on rubber heads and he was looking for his hand, which was shy due to its nudity, pointed to his temple with its index, and he would start laughing, alone behind the wheel. Oh! How he loved this autumn day when the cold seemed to come from the blinding sun! Lost, parked, his nose buried in maps, he looked up to see an Oriental walking towards the car as if she was the location he was looking for on the millimeter grid. At almost twenty years of age, she was short, tanned and dressed in dirty jeans and a pink scarf holding her frizzy hair up over her doe eyes.

She leaned on his car door. Yes, she knew the neighborhood well. She agreed to be his guide. She turned around and let out a cry. Her three companions came out from behind the truck. All quite young. Abdoul wanted to study engineering. Sélim was a guitar playing road worker and Saif, the strongest, was a truck driver with a big mustache. Then there was Fatima, their "sister," who served as their German-English interpreter. Following their indication, Christophe quickly found himself in front of the address of Eckel und Schmidt Import-

Export: an apartment building with its windows blocked by plywood, unoccupied because it was too close to the wall.

This quivering had to stop. The instructions were not coming in basic or in German, but in French, through the fingers, through the mouth. He was drifting. The wind had turned. He was paddling towards the faraway cave where his parents were embracing each other in the dark. The scene that repulsed and fascinated him, that he could not see because they had abandoned him, but that he hoped to re-enact with two corpses, two piles of stacked bones like in Pompeii. He was ready to burst into flames at the briefest stop of the magnifying glass.

The lead given by O'Reilly stopped here. Christophe questioned a neighbor that was getting into his car. "Amerikanisch?" he asked him. Sportsman's running shoes. Tired, he did not clarify: Kanadischer. Why had this building been emptied? They closed that whole side of the road down. Too many tunnels. The last one even went through Hitler's old bunker. Where are the old tenants? At the post office, they should know.

Long wait in a monumental marble hall. The Post's Fräulein furrowed her brow and sighed impatiently and went to consult her superior. Long consultation in low voices over big notebooks. "We do not have a forwarding address," she said as she came back to perch on her stool.

"And their mail?"

"We keep here for two weeks. They can pick up the remaining mail."

Better than a PO Box, Christophe thought as he turned back. The Turks have to go back to the West after having their transit visas renewed by the East-German authorities. "A hundred marks every time," Fatima told him. "If we don't have a job next time, they'll surely send us back to Ankara." She looked at him, her eyes full of hope. He thought of hiring her as a guide and interpreter for a moment. Maybe. For now, he only wanted one thing: to go to bed to make up for the lack of sleep.

He dropped them off at a subway station. Fatima invited him to visit her in Kreutzberg. When he was about to fall asleep, Christophe saw von Chénier enter his room, dressed in a richly decorated suit. His face in the shadows. Egging him on in a soft voice to continue his research. Lifting the golden strike of a Kronenbourg to his health, its buck shimmering on the bedside table's yellow tablecloth. I wanted to conquer this city, his father explained. Between the two of us, we still can. I want you to give me my peace, and for you to restore the honor of our name. But he, Christophe, had no son. When he would die, everything that was confined in his memory would disappear, including the present. Those faces that brush by in staircases or when gazes cross each other like leaves the bad weather would blow away. Here, in this bed, he was looking at himself, the pale hero of an unborn nation.

The next day, he found Fatima in a furnished room of Kreutzberg where she lived alone. The air was cold, despite the incandescent coil of a heater. She was freezing in her t-shirt that fell over her tapered jeans which left her ankles naked, as she rubbed her round mouth with her wrists sporting many cheap quartz watches like bracelets. Tiny tin staples pinched her ears. Her big eyes widened beneath the scarf that cleared her forehead.

"Can you come with me to the grocery store?" she asked.

A great force suddenly possessed him. The time of fluid hesitation and visceral anguish was over! He was becoming a tiger, his stride lengthened; he felt he would be able to kill in joy. He knocked a pebble with his foot: it hit a red tulip that shook and lost a petal.

On the wet grass, the shadow of an oak was sinking in the lamppost's light. As he went forward, the branches moved to the left. He tightened his fists in his blazer, protective nest of Italian leather, around his navel, behind which that beast was leading him to follow this Ottoman that rocked her hips on the overly high heels of her cowboy boots. She turned and smiled at him with her small, regular teeth. He was carrying pineapples and two cartons of milk in a plastic bag.

How could he court a twenty-four year-old Turkish girl who just had to close her eyes to be in Ankara, in the great villa her father Colonel Saïd Nursi built behind the Atatürk Mausoleum, and in her ears the trumpets of the guard relief in front of the square column? He felt a prickle on his lips, like after anesthesia. Fatima appeared in a spark of intensity, a reality that tore tears of admiration from him. She was lying on her bed. His hands fell on her like gulls on the sea, she said again, and his pleasure began to rise.

In the morning, he explained that he needed an interpreter to help him in the research he intended to do on a Canadian historical figure: André Chénier, also known by the name of von Chénier who died in Berlin in 1945. They would have to consult archives. Contact different ministries.

"Who is he to you?" she asked.

"My father, a man who made a mistake. And who tried to redeem himself."

"When a father gets lost," she replied looking at him intently, "it's often with his son, no?"

They fought against a freezing wind to go eat at the Kurfürstendamm McDonald's. "In Gogol's *Dead Souls*," he told Fatima, "there is a

Russian character named MacDonald." He swallowed the meat patty. "Ite missa est."

They were telling each other the humiliations of their respective people while researching the halls of the ministry, inquiring with certain government agents, photocopying documents and examining the area's city plans.

"I'm thirty years younger than you," she was saying. "But you're naïve! Blond, thin and hard. Like the blade of a knife. Like a boy I loved in Ankara. The same metallic gaze. He planted bombs, too. His exploded between his hands. In an airport. He was a Shiite. Because of him, I can't go back to finish medical school. I've been labeled a terrorist."

To cheer him up, she dragged him on the Kurfürstendamm, where they listened to the city's neo-Babylonian twitter, watching for its ghosts. In the discos, the pink fluorescents snaked over the dancers; the waitress rocked her hips against the cash register. Immense heartbroken city, but with a stomach of steel that could swallow everyone. Check, please! Sign it! "Everybody is signing it!" said Fatima, leaning on a plastic palm tree, dressed in a jacket made of two pieces joined together by laces on either side. When she bent forward to light up from Christophe's lighter, he could peek at her left breast.

"Don't hesitate to become a killer," she told him, "take anyone and twist their neck. In school, I defended my ideas with scissors." She climbed the ladder that led to the dance floor, and every sway of her hips, forced by her too tight skirt, showed him the line of her pantyhose which followed the curve of her thighs under the fabric, up to the next line, more secret.

It opened the path of his desire.

She cried to him over the music: "Don't think about all those who are dead. Do you know what they want from you? That you taste, that you enjoy and tell them all about it."

She explained she was looking for a country of refuge. What did he have to offer her? She caressed the nape of his neck. "You could get me into Canada?" she asked. He burst into laughter as he unbuttoned her dress. He laid his head on her chest and plugged his ears with her patchouli-scented breasts. Ready to commit crimes to caress her mane falling on her back that made him salivate.

He had left his hotel to go live with her in Kreutzberg. The laundry hung heavily on the line pulled between the pole of the stairs and the tall poplar, its leaves quivering. The alley's asphalt was warped, wrinkled with frozen black waves. A filter covered the sky, where violet clouds snaked like caterpillars spinning their cocoons, wrapping Berlin in a silk he hoped was indestructible. The images needed a new setting, that of dreams. He fell asleep while listening to the falling rain.

NOTEBOOK THREE

At the age of seventy-five, Ernst Hofer was cruelly disappointed with life. His pharmaceutical laboratory's patents fell into public property, so he could not receive any more royalties for the medicine created by Jewish chemists whose creativity he had stimulated by keeping them away from the camps long enough to harvest the fruits of his generosity. Harnessed by a few miracle remedies, these Jews had allowed him to live in luxury in his Corinthian column villa of Tempelhof, bought in 1953 from an Old South American general.

Unfortunately, the political demon still possessed him so that, during those years of abundance, instead of investing it all in Krupp or BMW, he had funded a publishing house that specialized in tales of old torturers disguised as noble heroes of the Eastern Front. But, from the Israeli grey cells, there was no juice left to squeeze. To refill his safe, he had counted on a contract with the Pentagon, which wanted to stock up on suicide pills for likely survivors of a nuclear conflict. But a senator questioned the political background of the president of the Swiss firm that held the patents. A Jew, of course! Persecution against Germany would seemingly never cease!

Hofer believed he was not condemned to poverty, but to mediocrity, like Mengele and Eichmann before their deaths, brought back to their original situation of frustrated and dull little bourgeois. He had vowed for a long time to avoid this pathetic fate, even if the price was a Wagnerian suicide that would turn his house into a funeral stake. But with age he considered surviving even on a more modest lifestyle.

In reality, he was still a multimillionaire, in dollars and in marks, but in his mind, his fortune could only decline because it was not increasing. Without admitting it, he thought his existence would not end as long as his assets remained inexhaustible. He, he thought while sighing, who had almost become viceroy of Quebec, absolute master of a whole population, would then have to end his days in a seedy furnished Kreutzberg apartment? No! He felt that his salvation would come from his distant imaginary empire when he read in a Canadian magazine, he was stubbornly still subscribed to, that the Helgoland – renamed Pickle in a blasphemous way – would be auctioned off at the beginning of June, in the Halifax port.

He remembered the microfilms he had hidden onboard so carefully, so that when they shipwrecked he did not have time to retrieve them. No one had discovered them, because the crowd he still moved in would have quickly learned about the appearance of documents from the Führerbunker.

The money he wired to O'Reilly would have raked in a hundredfold if the microfilms had not contained, after examination, unsigned trivial dispatches, addressed to the troops defending the Zitadelle Berlin. Without any commercial value on the Black Market of Nazi souvenirs. This transaction cost him a few ten thousand marks, but he came to the conclusion that von Chénier had sabotaged the microfilming operation and that the notebooks in which Hitler scribbled on his last days were still at the bottom, in the secret bunker the Russian had never detected, beneath the official bunker that they had blown up in 1947.

Found in the trunks of an old deceased GI, a photo album of the Führer's childhood had sold for four hundred thousand dollars. And for the fake Hitler souvenirs? The Spiegel had paid six million marks. Graphologists all agreed on its authenticity: written by the Führer's hand, with the appropriate shaking after the explosion of Colonel Stauffenberg's bomb, they said. But no one questioned how he could have aligned entire armies of words when his tank divisions were in disarray. After some chemical and spectrographic analysis, it was found that the notebooks had been made in 1980. On Canadian paper no less.

Then came the joke between editors at the Frankfurt Fair, in October: who had spit and for how much? For a Mengele exhumed from the cemetery, what a laugh: Bormann was growing melons in Bolivia, Gœbbels on a ranch in Colorado. But how much would a handwritten and unpublished notebook of the Fürhrer sell for? Just thinking about it made him shiver with delight. There remained the delicate issue of retrieving said manuscript.

At that moment, von Chénier's son arrived in Berlin and was yelling in the prefecture and Senate halls, demanding to know what had happened to his father forty years earlier. Through his network of old comrades of the Propaganda Ministry, he easily obtained the name of the hotel where the new owner of the Helgoland claimed he could be reached. He was tempted to order for this hornet to be squashed, for if it buzzed around too much over a few dead bodies it might sting the Canadian Press' curiosity. Even today, an investigation on Perceval Perkins' accidental death would bother him, especially with the absence of a protective and cheating policeman like Dansereau. Publicity, trial, deportation: the script was unfortunately too well known and often ended in Jerusalem.

But before getting rid of him, he wanted place this importune Canadian visitor to contribution. He intended to inspire himself from the terribly efficient lazy executioner's method: asking the victim to dig his own grave. For he thought that truth was a corpse-like stillness of the last brain cell, rotting away on a sample slate under a Nobel Prize microscope.

NOTEBOOK FOUR

"What?" Christophe cried out drawing out the Prussian government agents with Fatima's help, "You can't find my father André Chénier's work files? What a scandal! He worked for your government for six years. We're convinced, my family and I, that he didn't receive his full wages. And unless you have proof of the contrary, we will file a lawsuit to regain what is owed. We will also notify our embassy to get war compensations."

He was bluffing. His cause, no international tribunal would so much as receive it. But he hoped to raise the bait this way. And two weeks after his arrival in Berlin, on a Sunday morning, he received a telephone call from a certain Hofer.

"I learned, through friends of mine, that you were looking for information on von Chénier? Your father, nein? I would like to help you. I knew him a little and I called him a friend."

He arranged to meet for breakfast at a café in the Tiergarten. Who was this Hofer? An innocent bystander, a simple colleague or the "German friend" Virginia had told him about? Impossible to know without exposing himself to danger, like an x-ray. Christophe dressed with care as meticulous as the bullfighters before the corrida. On his wrist glistened eighteen-karat wrist cuffs; he pierced his black tie with a ruby that glowed a fiery red on his dickey between the lapels of his Maxim chevron suit.

Fatima seemed intimidated; she had only seen her lover wear jeans, which her own wardrobe consisted of. Since she insisted on coming along, he used the excuse of their clothing incongruity to ask her to wait in the car. In reality, he preferred that Hofer did not lay eyes on her.

After a few minutes of wandering on the roads of the immense park behind the wheel of the Opel, he found the restaurant: a hunting lodge with wide bay windows. He parked a little bit further, behind a grove of pines.

A waiter showed him to the table where Hofer was talking into a mobile phone that was held by a chauffeur wearing a livery, immobile in front of a single cover. Raven black hair surely dyed at his age. His ink black eyes held flashes of pure ruse; he moistened his right index with his tongue and slicked his bushy eyebrows. He hung up, and then took a napkin that the other tied around his neck. Christophe moved closer.

"Herr Hofer?"

"Monsieur Chénier!"

A heavy and compact voice. On the dining room wallpaper violets slowly fell. He stood up. An American handshake rather than a bow like in the North.

"It is such a pleasure to see the son of an old friend. You look a great deal like your father. A little older, obviously, since the poor man disappeared at such a young age. Sit down and let us see if I can help you."

As he spoke, he pinched his trumpet, broken-veined nose with its bulb-like end, and he moved his protruding chin.

"I'm trying to piece together the life of my parents who were here back then," Christophe said. "I have undertaken the task of writing my father's biography. Not an easy thing without documents or witnesses."

Hofer listened, his hands on his lightly full stomach and, slipping his feet out of his loafers, he rocked himself lightly, nearly making himself fall asleep. He exhaled roughly and swallowed his drink in one swoop: a mix of cola and rye, furiously shaking the ice that was left, and the waiter hurried over with another glass.

"Prosit!" Hofer lifted his glass, studying him from behind his yellowish cornea. "And so you are interested in your father, of course. You, at the time, a little angel in your peaceful igloo... Von Chénier. Raised by your grandmother after your uncle Perceval's death? Let us continue in French. Your German..." He sighed. "and your Canadian accent bring back so many memories. I followed your political life. Your nationalist parties: no more luck than your father in his time. Your country, we cannot catch by the left or by the right. And you? Divorced without children? The line will stop here then. A pity. Me, business is killing me, crucifying me. No, worse, because then again, that would be a normal situation..."

He spread his arms and cocked his head to the side.

"But disjointed, dismembered in grotesque positions, until the opponents make minced meat out of me. When the mark becomes flesh, what happens? An upside-down crucifixion? A swastika? You do not smoke?" His chauffeur lit a cigar for him. "So you are a translator, I think? You are making a decent living?"

"I limit my spending."

Hofer burst into a booming laughter. "That is German humor, that. Very good!"
He stopped to pour a pink vial in his drink. "My invention. Hoferium," he said. "A light dose creates euphoria, a heavy dose 'euthanizes.' Smell it!" Smells of chlorine. He blew over the vial's opened tip. A low key. "The Pentagon will need it to spare the American population agonizing radioactive pain. Really, the Nazis were children. Now we do a lot better. With less noise, but much better. Hoferium will be the chemical wafer of the real god: death, nein?"

Outside, near the duck pond, three whores, mini-skirts slit up to their butts, were sucking their thumbs. Fatima lowered the car window. In the distance the lights of Berlin were shining up to the great shadow zone to the East. A silence.

"I cannot really give you any information. Your father worked for me, but I rarely met him, only during service meetings. I saw him again toward the last days. I had gone to the bunker to receive orders from my boss, Doctor Gœbbels, a charming man, you know, and so educated. There was no moon when I arrived. Your parents were standing at the entrance, near the ventilation tower. We had just built it to protect the ventilation system from gas grenades. With its cone-shaped roof, it looked like Méliès' rocket in 'A Trip to the Moon.' Your father said to me: 'A shame we can't get it to take off.'

"All the Berliners wanted was to escape the surrounding. On the other hand, all our foreign collaborators, like your father, flowed back to the center, because to capture them meant the firing squad, and the chancellery defended its last perimeter with French SS from the Charlemagne division.

"You parents looked exhausted. Especially your father, whose vocal organ, that tenor one on our radio, had become a mere hoarse thread. I asked him how long he planned to stay. 'Until the end. Actually, I don't have a choice,' he whispered while pointing to a guard that was keeping his eyes on us. He dragged me a bit further away and whispered even more quietly: 'There's a bunker beneath the bunker. That's where they plan to wait out the storm before fleeing.' "

We talked for a while, then he hit the notebook he was holding against his chest with the palm of his hand. "I used the rest of my strength to write my memoirs."

"Even in that end of the world decor, your mother shone so much that Eva Braun was jealous. She was worried about the winter crows that usually stopped in Berlin when they migrated that year and had almost all passed over the city without stopping. The ones that had the bad idea of landing littered the streets with their bullet-riddled bodies or they would turn into distraught and noisy swarms. Lizbeth hated herself for dragging her husband in this unfortunate adventure."

Hofer's eyes brimmed with tears as he seemed to hesitate, moved.

"Just before one of the guards brought him back towards the metal staircase that went underground, von Chénier said to me: "I wrote my story so that my son Christophe could learn the truth about me." That is why, my dear, I wanted to meet with you this much: I have a message to give you…"

Slowly, the room was filling up with customers wearing Tyrolean. Schuppmann, the chauffeur, had left them, perched on a stool, his boxer face leaning over the bar made of nickel; he was gargling his Schnapps as if he was about to spit it on his reflection. Fatima was talking with one of the whores posted at the entrance of the wooden path. Christophe's apprehension melted away bit by bit as the other presented his parents in a more sympathetic light.

Hofer looked at his watch. "Would you have a bit more time to give to a poor old man? I would like to make you visit a place that would surely interest you."

Christophe agreed. The other folded a fifty-mark bank note lengthwise and placed it on the bill. Sitting behind the wheel of the Opel, Fatima had the reflex to ignore them when they left, but she followed the heavy Mercedes smoothly driven by Schuppmann. They stopped about a hundred meters before Checkpoint Charlie. Hofer and his guest went up a public sightseeing turret. Wooden stairs, three flights without risers, a shaky, badly sanded handrail, then a fragile platform of loose planks, soiled by the soles of visitors.

When they lifted their eyes up in the wind that brought out tears, their gaze met with the first wall and its delirium of graffiti; then, below them, the no man's land with its barbwire and it's anti-tank barricades that spiked up in the concrete dust coming from the fortifications: watchtowers in staggered rows punctuated with bay windows that reflected the clouds, sentry booths where sentinels stomped their feet.

Hofer showed him a slight hill in the forbidden space between the two walls. "Underneath, there is the Führerbunker," he said. "The Russians blew up the access way in 1947 and they leveled the ground. In 1966, a Western Berliner dug all the way there to allow his family to escape to the Soviet side. What did he see? Hitler, with his German Shepherd he was never able to train, reading the Spiegel and watching a football game on TV, Nuremberg versus Hanover? Living without food or air, writing his apocryphal memoirs? I was a kid, of course. But if your father told me the truth, the third bunker should be hidden under there, beneath the two subterranean levels the Russians found. And I do not want to sadden you, but you will surely find the remains of your parents there, and also maybe, your father's memoirs."

They went back down. Some punks were roasting sausages on a grill and greeted them by nonchalantly lifting their arms. "Sieg heil!" These words, spoken in a low voice, echoed as if a crowd were cheering.

"I will be honest with you," Hofer continued as they walked along the wall on a bushy path, littered with beer cans and yellow Kodacolor wrappings. "Your case interests me in a purely commercial sense. I have a small publishing house that is not doing very well at the moment, but that I could boost with the publication of von Chénier's journal, as well as your tale if you are able to fool the Russians by digging a tunnel right under their noses. We, Germans, love to get revenge with pranks of the sort. Our young aviator that landed his Cessna on the Red Square gained a fortune."

Schuppman was following them in the Mercedes. Fatima remained invisible. Had she abandoned her stalking? They arrived in front of a blue Prussian villa with three floors to let, cracked from the bad weather. Empty in expectation of a buyer that would renovate it or more likely, tear it down. Alone in the middle of a wasteland.

"There. I am proposing a clandestine archaeological dig. Here, behind the coach door, a garden that would give the site all the privacy it needs. The police prefecture will not bother us; I still have old friends there. People are still digging dozens of tunnels beneath the wall. From the East to the West, which actually presents more risk than our project, since we are not aiming to come back up to the surface, but instead we would stay down in the crypt beneath the Soviet zone. We could pretend we are digging up the villa to build a disco, that would be named the Führerbunker, just like Hitler's refuge located nearby. It will give the tourists as well as the Berliners, a chill. The barmen would be dressed as Adolf, in uniforms with steel crosses and little moustaches. We would play heavy metal."

"Fifty-fifty?" Christophe asked. "Spending and profits?"

Schuppmann was not following them aboard the Mercedes anymore. Christophe wondered why, and then shrugged his shoulders. They wrote down the agency's number written on the rental sign and headed towards the café around the corner to make a phone call. The owner wanted a three-month lease, at two thousand marks per month, payable in advance. They sat in a corner drinking beer. Two griffins opened their protective wings over the bar's bottles. The short waitress in a purple jumpsuit pretending like she was boxing a patron, on the giant screen, the heroine of a soap was sending a distress call on her CB. Too late: the minivan was falling and exploding at the bottom of a ravine. A UVA tanned client dropped her dirty jeans on a stool and ordered a Pils as the WC's bowls talked to each other by moving their lids like jaws.

There. They had found the basis of their operation. They had made the calculations: a hundred and fifty meters to cover, twenty dollars for every meter of tunnel. In total: twenty thousand dollars, with half for Christophe. His entire fortune! He would have to open an account in a bank in Berlin.

"We could become associates by creating a company..." Hofer said.

"That we would call Eckel und Schmidt Import-Export," Christophe said, who still did not trust his companion. But hearing the name of a company that had tried to purchase the Helgoland, the other did not flinch. "The name matters not," he said, not lifting his eyes from the paper where he had begun to list all the material needed.

At that moment, with a haggard look, Fatima entered the room, miniscule next to the huge Schuppmann that was leading her by the elbow.

"Do you know this girl?" he asked Christophe.

"Yes. Let her go!"

The chauffeur silently questioned his boss who blinked slowly as a sign of agreement. Fatima snuggled next to Christophe who had stood up and was sizing Schuppmann with his eyes.

"Did he hurt you?" he asked.

She shook her head and smiled bravely.

"I am sorry, miss," Hofer said. "I noticed that you had been following us from the restaurant a little while ago. I wanted to know why. Here, in Germany, with all the terrorists, businessmen have to take extra care. Come sit with us, please."

Christophe hesitated. Twenty years earlier, he would have tried to break his chair on the chauffeur's black cap without thinking. But Fatima lightened the mood by answering Hofer.

"Christophe hired me as a guide and interpreter. I did not want to bother the private nature of your meeting, but I did not realize that my behavior could seem suspicious. My name is Fatima."

Christophe did the introductions and the four of them ended up around the solid oak table.

"Istanbul?" Hofer asked.

"No. Ankara."

"Oh? Do you know who drew the plans of your city? Jansen, a Berliner who inspired Speer with Hitler's new chancellery. It stood exactly where we are now. Monsieur Chénier and I have decided to become partners in the practice of historical digs in the neighborhood. We will need a few workers. Would you know any compatriots it might interest? We would pay cash and would not ask any questions."

"I can give you a few names."

"Very good. You will see to that with Christophe. You will live on site, in the pension. We will save money that way."

"Tomb raider!" This insult of the Egyptian archaeologists toward the pharaoh looters, Christophe addressed himself as the conversation went on about practical organization of the future site. Underneath the flooring swept by a black sleepy waitress with sawdust, were possibly hidden irrefutable traces of his past, partially disintegrated by the winds of treasons. He felt the same uncontrollable nervous excitement as he did at the moment of his attacks. In this instant, he was not defying the federal state of Canada, but the four powers of the Berlin occupation. For a futile and microscopic reason within history: learning the fate of his parents. And the identity of their killer. Who still lived, and was laughing in his beard, if he even had one, rather than a shaven face like Hofer's.

"If our research is conclusive before the Book Fair in Frankfurt in October," the editor declared, "we could rent a plane for the serious customers and let them visit the Führerbunker. When given a chill, the Americans quickly bring out their checkbooks."

Fatima was slowly recuperating from the fright she got when Schuppmann had seized her by the arm while she had been waiting in front of the café. She thought he was part of the law enforcement until he brought her to a small room, in front of the old man whose opaque gaze made a scorpion run up the back of her neck.

When Hofer left them, Christophe ran to the café's urinal. Oppressed, he splashed his forehead with water. Both faucets bore the letter H, engraved in cursive style with baroque embellishments, thus falsely indicating with the abbreviations H H (heiss, heiss) two jets of hot water. As he fixed his hair, he could not recognize himself, as though he were wearing a sinister mask. He thought that the real flaw in all the stories of pacts with the devil was that they assumed the prince of lies was coming forth with his real name.

NOTEBOOK FIVE

The abandoned hostel that Christopher and Hofer rented from September second stood fifty meters away from the wall of Potsdamer Square and, beneath it, the Führerbunker; in the middle of the wasteland full of cast-iron bathtubs that floated under the streetlights. As a means of protection against vandalism, the windows were heavily boarded up, except on the fourth and final floor. Daylight penetrated the rooms only through the backyard where the spiral staircase rose, lit by light shelves on the right of the path that lead to the coach door,

Christophe had moved in with Fatima under the attic, in an empty and echoing room. A Venetian blind hid him from the guards in the watchtower, on the other side of the wall. He often watched the official cars that passed the Eastern-Western border at Checkpoint Charlie with binoculars, on the American military convoys that went along the wall: dozens of trucks, Jeeps, trailers spiked with antennas, full of containers, covered in camouflage print tarps with numbers written in chalk over them. On Radio-Moscow, a French feminine voice spoke in monotone about the "Palestinian students that had walked in the streets of Jerusalem while chanting slogans demanding the immediate departure of the occupation forces."

Aside for a few heavy and scratched mahogany pieces of furniture, Bauhaus style, there only remained a few tens of thousands of paperback novels from the deceased owner's library; all worthless. Everywhere, in the halls, in the dining room with oak paneling, in the bedrooms and even on the staircase walls, the obscure books lined up as fine as the ones that had covered Pompeii right before the lava came down.

He had not properly closed the shower curtain so water was splashing on the tile floor where the ceiling light erased all traces of dawn. He could not find the towels; he had surely thrown them at the back of a closet, where the smell of mold would eventually grab his attention. For now, he was drying off with his bathrobe. When he exited the bathroom, his watch was beginning to defog: six o'clock. The first bus was already moaning.

So, as to not wake Fatima up – she was still sleeping – he dressed in the dark, knowing where his clothes were around him. He was an orderly man. He went down the stairs and found himself in the yard where they could, for now, easily hide the earth coming from the excavation.

The rain was showering down Christophe's black Opel, as well as the tools scattered around the well that was covered with linoleum. Crouched on a squared pile of lumber, Abdoul was smoking while he waited, a shovel in his hand. His black hat down on his ears, he hummed in Arabic. "Boss, we dug fifty meters yesterday. You happy?" he asked. "Where are the others?"

"They'll be here right away."

"The Turks only understand kicks in the ass!" Schuppmann said in a sharp and precise voice. He lived with them to protect Hofer's interest, calling him every day. Shirtless and powerful, he blew his nose as he stood in the door of the old janitor's lodgings, where he slept with his weights, which he would not stop lifting according to a body builder's choreography, in which steel replaces woman as a partner. He had given some explanations to a police patrol a few days earlier, but his contribution to the work site stopped there: he hated physical labor that might harm his astonishingly white and delicate hands.

Abdoul spit in his direction and got up when Selim, the skinny guitar player, and Saïf, the mustached truck driver, arrived. They removed the tarp, uncovering the ladder and the well that led to the end of the tunnel. In their advance towards the Führerbunker, they were now progressing under the zone protected by machine guns with acoustic triggers that threw steel cubes at the slightest sound. With their shovels, they dug frantically for ten marks per meter. The sandy soil did not cave in. They were treading in several centimeters of water. It was cold and humid. They caught colds with fevers. Christophe himself was suffering from laryngitis. When he cracked and fainted, the others pulled him by the legs up to the ladder at the bottom of the well.

They took turns every other hour. Abdoul, who had a friend working at a slaughterhouse, was able to get tinplate containers. Each container could hold one hundred and fifty pounds of sand and soil. The worker removed the soil and packed it in the containers. He had to fill up fifteen times before trading shifts with someone else. Sometimes they would hear the Vopos patrolling over them and they would stop. Despite the freezing cold, they all wore jeans and short-sleeved shirts.

At night, Fatima would tell him he smelled of soil, das Erd, in her tongue, which she would slide over his volcanic stomach, the saliva leaving a trail of vapor below his navel. He came, his sperm leaked in the tunnel, stimulating the digging work, throwing itself like an acid assaulting the last obstacles separating him from Hitler's illuminated form, still scratching his pen on the lined pages of the notebooks he had bought in Vienna with his friend Kubizek, as he was already dreaming of building a new opera house in the city of Linz, but the ground was catching up with Christophe with its steel teeth, he could not move this frigid earth anymore.

Fatima was worried. Christophe liked this earth and the silence around him too much. He was slowly giving up on the world of the living for that of the dead.

"You'll take me to Canada tomorrow?" she asked as she leaned her elbows next to his on the windowsill. She imagined the wall in front of them was a huge mirror that was sending back to them a reversed image of the city, reflecting the towers, the cars, the buses, imprinting them with a silence that was reminiscent of the country, under the bulb like the tip of the DDR television antenna, as if the whole of Berlin was a show being broadcast permanently in their brains .

She spoke to him softly, in this French she had begun to learn from him: murmured sounds, whispered against the night's ear. "No word is sensible, not even the most humble, the most reassuring. They are all shaking in anxiety, repeating I am not dead, no, not yet, since I still talk."

It was raining outside; the wind was chasing the newspapers that the lazy neighbors had left outside the door, up the wall. The news travels fast, as they say, and the photo of a terrorist can be seen on the front page, with the promise of reward. Christophe recognized Abdoul. No one picked up the paper that then fell in a puddle where the ink ran.

Always faithful to his promise to publish the chronicles about the dig site, Hofer had lent him a microcomputer to send his text directly to the reviser with the description of discovering the Führerbunker. When Christophe sat in front of the keyboard, he felt like he was being tortured to write. A shiver ran through him and the slash of a sword cut his abdomen open; he could not breathe anymore. Then, Fatima would kneel in front of his wound, kiss it and bandage it. Berlin did stand for any such barking in front of its wall. They made love. What a machine, all contact, breath, weight and counterweight! The room shifted behind the arched nape of his neck.

Fatima Nursi felt that her Quebecer lover was slipping away from her, not to the scented hands of another woman, but to the dubious prestige of death, which, stuck to Christophe's heels and under his nails, his hair and, it seemed to her, behind his dull and absent gaze, was now spreading its odor of festering mud even into their bed. She, who had known how to fight for the rights of Kurds and women, who had eight lawsuits hanging over her head for a total of forty-five years in prison, remained powerless in front of the melancholy that she felt was inspired by Christophe's past – digging the maternal soil of Berlin, was he not trying to rewind the course of time up to the time of his birth, his separation from Lizbeth – of which he had no memory?

And when she asked him to describe his country – to distract him as well as to get information for herself on this America where she planned to find refuge at the end of September when the German authorities would want to deport her back to Ankara – he talked to her about the snow banks his compatriots had to plough to get around. "Snow, it's nothing, it's void that we spend our lives moving around between two short summers. Our only national palace is the ice palace of the Quebec Winter Carnival."

He quoted mad poets; authors who had committed suicide, all bards of this people one half of who, after the defeat, accused the other half of treason. The sun warmed the Spree being patrolled by the RDA gunboats, and where the watchtowers were reflected. She looked at his face wound up in thought, wrinkled around the lips, the ones of a seducer who refuses to grow old.

He had hoped to give birth to himself in the crude lights of the being, with the forceps of his mind; but he was giving in to the vertigo of the void, inspired by the biggest lack of history of the world.

"Was ist Kebek: ein Mus oder ein Muss? Marmalade or necessity?" he asked himself, chuckling. "My father believed we were vanquished. But there was no defeat because there was no battle. And no battle because there was no country to defend."

What could she answer him? She felt that only actions would reach him. At night, they would join up in the yard, around a fire, beneath the starlit rectangle cut by the lead gutters. Slim Selim was playing the guitar, Saïf-the-mustache was telling stories of his wild runs on the road between Teheran and Ankara, in the mountains where the villagers ransomed the truck drivers by forcing them to pay 'insurance' on the broken windshields and the flat tires and Abdoul, the engineer-dirt digger who was wanted by the police, was calculating the number of support beams they would need for the next day.

They spoke in the bastardly language of their group: of Ankara, the "Grey Wolves," the Turkish fascists. They spoke of baklava, shish kebab, goat's cheese, the Prophet. But mostly, they talked about the Helgoland.

Fatima participated in the dig by spreading the containers of soil throughout the rooms of the ground floor. Twice a day, she would bring them Big Macs in little styrofoam coffins. They all suffered from stomach cramps.

One afternoon, Christophe did not have the strength to go on, so he came back in earlier than planned. He found Fatima standing in the middle of their room, naked, her hands tied behind her back and a rope around her neck that was tied to one of the ceiling beams, which forced her to stand on the tip of her toes so as to not strangle herself. He untied the ropes as well as the towel around her mouth that prevented her from spitting out the ping-pong ball that served as a gag.

"Schuppmann?"

He had come in just as she was coming out of the shower. He had insisted on drying her off. The others couldn't hear her from the bottom of the tunnel. She had obeyed him, even allowing him to tie her up in that position. And finally, he had been content to watch her in silence. Then he left, saying he would be back right away.

Alone in his improvised gym – which smelled of sweat and varnish – Schuppmann was pushing away invisible images with his muscles. The others did the same. All of them lost in their thoughts, suffering for her. Every movement, whether repulsion or attraction, costs energy. His thoughts crumbled. Athletic nirvana. He did not have to sum himself up with the aesthetically rational synthesis of an 'I' anymore. He lifted his weights to achieve the impossible transcendence. Sterile hysteria that screamed in silence.

Total war ruled on the cover of Schuppmann's magazines where SS whipped women who docilely obeyed, clicking their heels, their bathrobes opened on their bras.

He was listening to rock music and did not hear Christophe come in. His hands covered in powdered chalk, he was lying on a bench, grabbing a weight held up by two forks behind his head so he could bench press. Christophe prevented him from lifting the supported weight in cantilever with his triceps – above his chest and elbows locked. In this position, a light pressure of his thumb exerted a greater force than that of the entire colossus, puffing and turning red.

The bar touched his nose and crashed down on his teeth, the enamel screeched under the engraved steel. With a start, he pushed the bar to his throat where it crushed his windpipe; then he used it as a handlebar to twist his head in every which way. His red face grimaced. Pity took hold of Christophe before this puppet with its wires cut off, with marshmallow hands clamped on his and he let him catch his breath. Behind them, the Turks, covered in mud, had come in, and Abdoul was holding a knife.

"Heraus!" he shouted to the German.

In the deserted street that led to the wall, Schuppmann turned to face them; they were waiting for him to get into his black BMW, arms pointing outward, hands joined at his belt, he pumped his pectorals and his trapeziums in a hideous tension that reached his bloody face. Then he slipped his black shirt back on and disappeared.

The weather was cooling down; the sun was setting behind the lace of the wall. A graffiti: "Seele Mörderer." Killer of souls. The pink flamingo flight of the clouds. And the dead pigeon, on the corner of the street, God, Theos, Deus, Christophe thought, everywhere it is always you that does not appear. Was he not his father's son, the personification of the mind: the end and the beginning of man?

They piled up the sidewalk, in front of the door, the pierced plates of the weights, the heaviest ones underneath, in two cone-shaped steel towers. Then on the phone, Christophe explained the incident to Hofer and told him that Schuppmann no longer had a place among them.

"He only wanted to have some fun!" the other answered, "You

should not have turned him away for such trivia. Who will represent me on the site?"

Christophe hung up. In the yard, the Turks were regrouping in silence.

"Herr Hofer," he announced to them, "has just informed me that he is no longer financing the dig. So I have no choice. I have to fire you."

That was the moment Fatima chose to go down the stairs and join her comrades.

NOTEBOOK SIX

As soon as he was alone, Christophe lifted the tarp that covered the entrance of the well and then went down. Above his head, the concrete had cracked over more than twenty meters. The hoarse, burning breath of the Soviet artillery. But the Führer, he was sleeping soundly. Two floors below.

Above, they had ultra-sound monitoring systems. Quiet! No pneumatic hammers. Shovels and wicker baskets. Like all the clandestine tunnel diggers. Suddenly his pick, which he was holding above his head, hit a substance as hard as a rock. He looked up in front of him and, in the glow of his lamp he saw a smooth and even surface. Touching it, he checked that it really was concrete. The ceiling of the bunker was six meters thick, but the sides, like this one, were about only fifty centimeters thick.

He recovered a vial of sulfuric acid, which he splashed the wall with. With a rag, he protected the lower part of his face from the vapors that stank of rotten eggs. Then he attacked. Lying on his back, his airways and his eyes burnt from the sulfur.

Suddenly, the steel bar slipped from his fingers: it had just come in contact with emptiness. He widened the wound in the dragon's flanks sleeping there for forty years. He was soon able to slide his torso in through the opening. He found himself halfway up a wall covered in blue and filthy tiles from Friesland. He rolled around on his stomach and let himself fall on the floor soiled in black ashes.

He inspected about thirty low-ceiling rooms, linked by narrow corridors, painted in rust brown, invaded by mold. He recognized the chancellor's private quarters: three big rooms grouped around a toilet and a bathroom.

He was wandering in an empty labyrinth. Before blowing up the access ways, the Russians had taken everything out: plumbing, electric wiring and furniture. The spiral staircase that led to the upper floor was blocked with rubble. The earth was taking back the space little by little, still commanded by Berlin's ghosts.

The vastness of the place made it difficult to find the secret bunker close to the Spree, beneath the others, known by historians and that led to the Foreign Affairs Ministry, to the garden, to the new chancellery and to the tower that protected the air vent of the ventilation system. The split that divided the East and the West spread right above his head. He let himself fall to the floor, prisoner of his own heat beat, in the smell of dead rats, contemplating the reflections of his acetylene lamp on the metallic buckles on his boots.

Statue without any devices or openings to talk, to eat, nothing that came in or out, full up to the top of it's skull, cold and hard. He was capsizing at the bar of the Helgoland, the hare was smiling against Berlin's night; he took out his watch and made an appointment with himself in a thousand years. He had forgotten the dice that would abolish chance, he was scratching the Prussian's belly, and he was c-sectioning Germany, ripping away its Cesar a thousand times deader than a god.

He swept his face that had fallen in dust in one swoop and he went back to his room in front of the computer Hofer had lent him; the disk was turning – clicks and purrs – and the text appeared on the screen. The absence of a manuscript rendered any handwriting analysis obsolete. These digitalized, magnetized, electronic words actually belong to an 8086 microprocessor, Palo Alto patented.

Walkman on his ears. In the middle of the labyrinth, the red Buddha was kissing the Goddess Kali. Outside, a garbage man was yelling as he hit the truck's container where he had just dumped the garbage bins. This story, he would tell it to the end. Like brass, he would let himself flow into the mold of the tale. Electronic Oedipus, he had dialogues with the Sphinx with a screen in front of him.

The telephone rang. It was Hofer. "Since you have not allowed me to leave Schuppmann on the perimeter to protect my interests, I have invited your lovely friend Fatima to my house. I think she misses you. So notify me when the work is done. Yes, I know the Turkish workers have left you. But Schuppmann tells me you are very strong. So cheer up…And do not forget to write down the story of your exploits. I do want to publish you."

Chénier put on his work gloves to avoid splinters. The humidity and the cold caught in his throat. Half crouched, he moved in the gallery that was lit by light bulbs every ten meters, minding the support beams and the electric wire stretched between them.

His boots made a suction noise on the clay soil. He soon had to crawl. No more extension cords for the light bulbs. He lit his way with a flashlight. In Plato's cavern, next to Hitler's tomb, the glaciers' coldness was numbing him. On his death, nothing would change; the world would stay the same. The camera would continue to roll. Then why was he afraid? Simply put: he was fear.

On the mirror on the Führerbunker's wall, he found teeth. This skeleton smiled and looked at him. Here he was in the office. Behind the frieze? They would have covered the joints in cement, which would explain the surreal cement truck on the photos taken by the Russian when they arrived.

He could not use explosives, which singularly slowed his work down. It was night outside. He would only stop to drink a little bit of coffee he had brought in a thermos. He widened the opening with a rock and climbing pick. His strikes on the wall began to sound hollow. Around two o'clock in the morning, he was able to slide in a crypt that was crossed by two steel bars embedded in the block that fit perfectly in the wall behind him.

On the ground, his lamp uncovered a rectangle of darkness. The ladder that allowed him to go down the hole had been pulled out and leaned against the wall. He let it slide until it touched the ground. He counted the steps out loud. "Fifty!" The echo sent back the number when he reached the end of his descent. He found himself at the entrance of a vast room: his light lost itself without touching the other side. Above, it illuminated the round arcs from which hung ochre stalactites. From everywhere came the smells of rotting plants, rancid meat: the digestion of earth.

A few steps, at first on spongy clay soil, then on finer sand were his boots that squeaked while leaving tracks of mud. His left shoulder hit an obstacle: he stepped back to look at an electrical generator. He cut the big rubber wires and came back a few minutes later from the tunnel with an extension cord mounted on a reel. When he was done wiring the dynamo, a few sparks flew and the turbines began to turn with a deep and rough snore at first, then, as they gained speed and the oil that was under pressure spread into the motor, with a regular high pitched whistle.

DCA floodlights lit up, weak but gaining in intensity, converging on a Tyrolean cottage, with a cathedral roof and a balcony supported by beams made of oak, built against the wall of the cave, on top of a slight slant, on concrete foundations. A speaker was playing the first measures of the Ride of the Valkyries.

He searched every nook and cranny of the cave without finding an exit. The lake was, after examination, actually a river, its subterranean current widening, and then sank into a pile of rubble that blocked the entrance of the tunnel towards the Spree, that could have been navigated with the inflatable boat Christophe was now moving forward on, his torso over the edge of the stern, searching the clear water, where he found no skeletons.

He headed back towards the cottage that was reflected in the lake. He came in the dining room: a pedestal table buried under empty cans and a gramophone, still playing some Wagner.

A pencil was placed on top of two notebooks, their black covers wrinkled from the humidity. He opened the first one that read: "I have decided to stop waiting for the opportune moment to talk. Because it will most likely never come."

It took a long time for him to finish reading. When he was done, he mechanically looked at the cuckoo clock that hung above the kitchen counter full of canned food, and then he remembered it had not worked in forty years.

"It really looks like time has stopped here, would you not say, dear partner?" Hofer said who, preceded by Schuppmann, had entered the cottage on the tip of his toes. The Kebek Gauleiter. Pale and shivering. Resembling the character described by von Chénier: perched on a balcony of Chateau Frontenac like a vampire ready to take flight, his chin brandished over a crowd of Quebecers waving flags with swastikas. In gothic on the title cards, his replies twitched in the dark.

"Where is Fatima?" Christophe asked.

"She is resting at my villa... I am a little cross with you for not inviting me to the opening of the crypt. Were we not to share the artifacts found in our digs? Will you allow me to read the notebooks after you are done?"

With a sigh, he sat down on a sofa that nearly collapsed under him. Schuppmann brought him the two manuscripts. He flipped through the first one and let out after a few seconds: "Four million marks!" But the other one seemed to surprise him. He turned and turned it around in his hands, deciphering a few passages here and there. After a long while, he leaned back into the couch and said, "So you already know who I am. A pity, I would have liked to surprise you myself. Only, this manuscript your father left leaves a few questions in the air. Allow me the pleasure of clearing them up for you."

He got up, opened a bottle with a molded label and filled two cut Bohemian crystal glasses monogrammed AH, and that had been placed upside down on a Bauhaus buffet, with vodka. Hofer and Schuppmann went bottoms up. Christophe took out a notepad and the pencil left by his father and started taking notes.

"When the emergency exit blew up, the Führer did not really have a choice. Your father killed Adolph Hitler. By forcing him to commit suicide. We caught up with Friedrich, your dear Lizbeth's brother. He paid. Your parents, I simply abandoned here, to let them realize the extent of the damage they had caused. And then I sailed with these microfilms that, I thought, contained the writings of our leader, towards Canada, to take care of your uncle Perceval. But again your father had betrayed me. When I recovered them last month, thanks to our common friend O'Reilly, I saw they contained documents of no interest. But here they are now… Finally!"

He slapped the notebook he was holding against his chest. "Thanks to you! To your determination! You are agreeable to me, Herr Chénier! In another time, we could have worked together. But I will oblige you not to write down what I am saying."

Stubbornly, Christophe lowered his head and continued to scribble. Hofer snapped his fingers. Schuppmann moved forward, enormous. "Schuppmann, explain to the gentleman…" Without a word, the other grabbed the pencil and planted it in Christophe's right palm. Vibrating in the flesh, like the arrow of a Sebastian. He pulled it out and the blood began to flow. The tip of the lead had broken and stayed beneath the flesh.

"Allow me, dear friend, to explain my method to you like I have previously done with your father. Your enemies, you mercilessly attack them, you scan them to find their weakness, then you push in the pen with precision in the shell's fault, without forgetting to say with a friendly smile 'Pardon me, dear neighbor, but I cannot do otherwise!' That is that famous vengeance that is said is better eaten cold."

Without adding a word, he left the Tyrolean cottage with Schuppmann and headed towards the end of the cave, towards the ladder for the steel footbridge. Once over there, he turned and shouted at Christophe who had followed them from a distance.

"The explosion later on will be that of the tunnel that leads to the hostel. For now, I am leaving you with electricity. Take advantage of it to listen to Wagner."

And Schuppmann pulled the ladder away. Christophe tried in vain to pull out the black dart next to his lifeline. The fragment continued to dig further. Pain crossed his arm. The lead was flowing into his bloodstream like the text of his father embodied in his.

Despite the slight delirium and pain that coursed through him, he kept the edge of reason intact, the sharpness still cutting through the reality in front of him, keeping his integrity between the two clamps. Suddenly, he noticed that the predicted explosion had not occurred. Slipping his father's notebook under his shirt, he began to climb up one of the steel pylons that supported the footbridge. His heart beat wildly.

He began to run, noticing as he did the sticks of dynamites that had been placed at the entrance of the bunker but that Hofer had not ignited. When he came out into the yard, he understood why.

Weighed down by the rain that had soaked his brown felt coat, Schuppmann lay on his back, away from the protection of the roof that hung over the yard. Christophe leaned over him and shook him. He recognized the smell of the hoferium chloride. Rigor mortis. Hofer must have prepared the euthanizing vodka earlier; to remain the sole owner of the notebooks.

The ascension to death surely had been pure bliss for Schuppmann, if his large smile that showed his and gave the impression he was savoring a huge joke was anything to go by. But why had Hofer neglected to blow up the tunnel behind him?

He pulled Schuppmann by the ankles. His jaws closed on air. The occipital scraped the gravel, tracing a sandy line up to the well. The rain became heavier, making the soil even more slippery.

Digging his feet on each side of the other's torso, he crouched to grab the lapel of his coat. His breath was fogging up. Flexing his biceps, he tore the body off the ground and threw it in front of him. A resounding splash indicated that he had reached the bottom of the flooded tunnel twenty meters below. He removed the ladder.

The downpour had stopped. In a few months, bulldozers would demolish this abandoned hotel. And they would build on this lot a gigantic German civilization Museum. While digging the foundations, they might stumble upon a corpse, but Berlin's basement was full of those. In the lavender patch where clouds were fraying, the sun reappeared, hitting the windows of the first floor at an angle and turning them into mirrors. On one of the panes, he saw the fleeting reflection of a face, like a white flash.

Someone was hiding in a room under the slate roof. Hofer? Someone that had surely been watching for some time, but that would not be able to avoid him when he went up to meet them, not even by going through a window in the façade that was blocked by solid sheets of plywood. Without haste, he followed the path, vaulted in arches and mounted with stone cartridges with bas-relief of the Prussian eagle, and that led to the coach door made of two heavy panels that he had locked. Then, he began his ascension of the spiral staircase.

Strangely calm. Was a murder what it took to calm him down? Yes, but only one- the one he was precisely about to commit. An execution rather, ordered by the jury of victims from the other side called to testify through his patient research as a lone detective.

On each floor, he locked the door of the hall that led to the rooms. Everywhere the smell of molding plaster and humid soil had replaced the lingering one of sauerkraut. He was shivering. He took off his rubber boots. A slash on his left thigh stiffened his leg and forced him to walk by pivoting on his right hip.

He spied the silence in the empty building: the creaking of a shutter on its hinges, the dull shock of a pigeon landing on a gutter, the howling of the wind beneath the roofing. The risers seemed to close in as a single vertical wall where only the twisted copper rods between the golden eyelets indicated the place you could step on. On the last floor, he moved with difficulty down the hall that seemed to climb according to an exponential curve up to the door of his apartment: scratched, purple and grey, pierced with a peephole. A fist to the plexus bent his torso.

He imagined Hofer lolled in his tassel armchair, ready to shoot him through the wooden panel as soon as he would see the handle turn. Walhalla would receive him. He would die with a weapon in his hand. He opened it with a jab of his elbow. At the end of his aim, he found his father, sitting on a wobbly chair, in front of the computer. Christophe recognized him from the photos, because of their brief encounter in Paspébiac in 1943, only remained a few words spoken in a foreign language on the beach, as an inflatable raft came out of the darkness into the bay, with two sailors and a Kriegsmarine officer onboard.

In the glow of the cathode screen, the twenty-five-year-old red head looked like a Pierrot from the moon. His father wore a white uniform decorated with the golden sign of the Propaganda Ministry. He hummed as he typed on the keyboard. From the cigarette hanging on the corner of his mouth fell ashes that were dangerous for the chips logic circuits.

Christophe got up and walked closer to read what the other was writing.

"I'm finishing this tale for you. You wanted to know what happened to us, your mother and I. We fled. She was able to meet with her brother. In the last moment's confusion, the discipline was crumbling. The Führer finally committed suicide. The men in charge of watching me and guarding the entrance of the subterranean river had deserted their post in inflatable rafts. They almost came across Lizbeth and Friedrich who were coming from the opposite direction."

Comfortably lolled in his couch, he put his feet up on the windowsill. He had his back to Christophe and spoke in the accent of Quebec City. A little annoying, with its twitching, his reflection in the window next to his.

"They left the patrol without saying a word. Then, they went up the current to the lake. They called me and I came out of my hiding place. We only had to blow up the tunnel behind us. Poor Friedrich: a random shot when we were crossing the American lines! We ended up in Portugal, then in Venezuela. We couldn't go back home. Everyone still believed me to be a traitor."

He unscrewed the thermos Christophe had brought from Montreal and spread Virginia's ashes in the flames that crackled on the fireplace.

"Stop crying. You're not alone. I, your father, your reason, I will take care of you. Don't worry. I love you. I won't order you to destroy yourself. I'll cradle you when you whimper. Light you up in the darkness. You think me mad to come back from the dead to talk to you like this, distinctly, out loud. Since I have to scream for you to hear me, I will. I'm not a jealous god that hides his face in the clouds. I understand your despair, that you would damn me. But when death is there, very close, you'll hear my voice again. I'll console you. I'll teach you that you are your own father and your own son. You don't have to

187

suffer from any flame, from any hell. And we will reform the broken, unlinked chain of all the sons with all the fathers."

"Lie down; your mother will bring you some aspirin." This tale was nothing but lies: Lizbeth had died with von Chénier, during the battle in Berlin; under circumstances he would never clarify.

And yet he obeyed. He closed his eyes. He heard the water flow from the tap, then the sound of high heels on the parquet floors. A cold hand touched his forehead. "But you're feverish! Here, swallow!" He heard a muffled explosion that shook the ground. He rose on his elbows and saw Fatima who was handing him a caplet. "The explosion, what was it?"

"Go look at the yard." He partially opened the curtains on the window: a thick cloud of dust was lifting from the tunnel's well.

"What are you doing here?"

"Hofer locked me up in his villa. I was scared, but he stayed courteous. Adboul and Saïf waited for him to leave with Schuppmann and they came to rescue me. When I came back here, you were raving in the room, covered in mud. The djinns wanted you to join them. The earth had to close up, like a wound that heals. And there was that accident! The tunnel wasn't very sturdy… Were you the one who killed Schuppmann?"

His little Hittite from the deep Anatolian gorges was pulling him away from the monsters only with her smile. To the ones you could not show, who screamed and contorted. That ran like magma behind the facemask.

The next day, he wrote one last time, using the computer Hofer lent him. The, he mailed the disk containing his tale and his father's to a Berlin editor. Maybe they would publish their little song, the two or three steps that had been taken with a little bit of grace, without mocking anyone, while listening to their own rhythm.

He splashed hot water on the lower part of his face, and then lathered with foam "closer to smoothness." The blade on his skin: seismograph of his feelings. On this Thanksgiving Sunday, he was able to shave without cutting himself for the first time in months. Then he threw the Sperry computer at the bottom of the well that Abdoul meticulously buried with dirt.

"We have to catch the big grey wolf by the tail," he said. Inside the Opel, he went to the posh neighborhood near the free University of Berlin. He closed the door soundlessly. The two lions at the entrance of the garden of Hofer's villa were covered in hemp tarps for winter. Between Sirius that shone above the slate roofing and the Mauser, precision weapon with a scope that weighed heavily on his shoulder, he guessed an obscure link.

He moved forward under the balcony with marble columns. Behind the partially opened windows, violently lit by a crystal chandelier, Hofer was wearing his old black uniform. He was alone in front of the mirror above the fireplace.

The von Chénier cell punished the enemies of the people, its gauleiters, even imaginary. The revolutionary violence was going to sew back together a history torn apart by chance. Christophe heard Hofer say: "Alas, father and mother, homeland, torrential rain, squalls, screams are only illusions. What good does it do to get attached to them? What good does it do to be afraid? It would be like looking at something that has no existence as if it had any."

To an assassin, the victim has no form, Hofer believed, remembering Schuppmann's agony. To see it, he only has to close his eyes and stop thinking about it. An emptiness that digs itself and sucks in, that is what it is. Only words give an appearance of shape to the chaos dreamt at night. Final thrust of life from the bottom of the abyss. If everything went faster, it would already be over.

And the dead passed in ever-tighter rows, as history lined them up. How could truth come from the lips, from these exposed muscles that moved from simple ticks, that nothing stopped, no repulsive blasphemy, no name of god or of the devil? In all directions, they weaved a web above the void with suctions, grimaces and smiles. Always the glottis pushing, blocking, breathing. Nothing binary.

Jewish bibles. A code that oozed ambiguity, which allowed for an infinite amount of positions between yes and no. But soon, he would give a new bible to the Hermann Antique representative, who had come from Munich with a signed check of four million marks. Enough to live in luxury until the age of ninety.

Under their peaches and cream skin, he thought, men are all monsters, watching for the next exposed throat, faces offered with a smile, the second the guard is brought down to strike with the speed and precision of a viper, to inject their poison: words. As soon as they can: bite, hold, hypnosis, delirium. I want you, I dominate you. I say nothing more. No more speech, only strikes and parries.

He heard the sound of a rifle being loaded. Suddenly, he noticed the confusion, the trap, and the disaster that would fall upon him. In the shadows, from the other side of the French windows, Christophe's face appeared. His mouth slightly frozen, as if under anesthesia, grimaced and showed teeth that were still intact, but the enamel was worn. His eyes were mere slits as he took aim with the Luger equipped with a silencer.

Hofer wanted to convince him in a soft voice to continue his research. Who really was his father? Why did I spare you at the hotel before? What really happened between Lizbeth and I, during my stay in Washington, in 1938, a year before you were born? He wanted to invent one last lie. Which he might have believed himself, since he had spared Christophe. But he did not have the leisure to do so. Already the other was pulling the trigger. Time for one more sentence:

"Ich bin dein Vater!" he shouted.

I am your father. Breathed from within. Complete trepanation, the brain exposed to the air in the skull. The world exposed itself. Illuminated by his death. Because, to stop Christophe, he had picked the wrong words, the ones that reminded the old hero of his encounter with von Chénier, on that beach of the Chaleurs Bay, just before the inflatable raft brought him to the submarine. He had bent down and had whispered that very sentence in his ear, the meaning of which Christophe never understood.

But now he remembered and he understood. No, Christophe thought. Neither this one nor the other, Perceval. Neither the English nor the German. But Chénier. The father he was choosing as he emptied the barrel trough the windowpane.

As he died, wrapping himself in a shroud with the sheer curtains before falling forward on the rug, Hofer had whispered a few other words in German. But Christophe had not listened to him. Passing his hand through the shattered window, he opened the lock and entered. Hitler's notebooks were on the chimney mantle, opened on a lectern like a sacred text. Without hesitating, he threw them into the flame.